This book is a work of fiction. Names, places, events and characters are fictitious in every regard. Any similarity to actual events or persons, living or dead, is purely coincidental.

Published by
Lydian Press 2017
Find us on the World Wide Web at
http://www.lydianpress.com

UNDENIABLE PASSION

SIX LESBIAN COUPLES GET A HAPPY ENDING

DALIA CRAIG

Lydian Press

CONTENTS

A RECKLESS AFFAIR

Until I encountered Sheridan Brooks, I'd never really believed in love at first sight. My common sense dismissed it as a myth, a clever ruse, perpetrated on the gullible by the purveyors of a particular style of slushy romantic fiction. Sheridan changed my mind forever. Although I didn't know then just how much of an effect she would have on my life.

* * * *

The meeting had already started when I slipped into a vacant seat at the very back of the conference room, for the monthly pep talk, hoping nobody would notice my tardiness. However, I hadn't reckoned on catching the eye of the new director of human resources.

She paused momentarily from her introductory speech to fix me with an impenetrable gaze. Heat immediately flooded my face and, in the thousandth of a second before she broke eye contact and continued speaking, I fell hopelessly in love with her.

The black and white photograph in the company magazine hadn't done her justice. I sat transfixed, unable to draw my gaze away from the disarmingly sexy woman standing on the platform flanked by the other directors. My heart fluttered helplessly, like a trapped butterfly, in my chest. The fact she was the only woman amongst half a dozen men made her stand out from the crowd but it was more than that. Sheridan Brooks had a body to die for, with a neat waist and curves in all the right places, all accentuated by a beautifully tailored dark-blue pin-stripe suit, and a vibrant emerald-green shirt. She wore her blonde hair feathered around her expertly made-up face, the short-cropped style enhanced her sculptured bone structure. From a distance, I couldn't make out the color of her eyes but imagined them fiery green to match her shirt.

Although I hung on the melodic resonance of Sheridan's voice, I took in very little of the content of her speech or that of Mathew Crossly, the director of operations, who followed her. I was far too busy wondering how to get her alone, naked, and begging me to fuck her, to concentrate on something as mundane as increasing productivity.

How I might achieve my aim, defied imagination. Being a junior copywriter in a global advertising agency, the only contact I ever had with anyone on the sixth floor was during the scramble for coffee after one of these monthly meetings. Still, nothing ventured, nothing gained, I had plan of sorts and just needed a little luck to make it work.

As soon as the meeting wound down, I made a dash for the refreshment table and armed myself with a large black coffee. I reckoned I had a little over five minutes to put my plan into operation before the directors departed, having gone through the motions of socializing with us underlings. I worked my way through the crowd to within touching distance of Ms. Brooks. Her intoxicating perfume filled the air and drew me even closer. Satisfied that I'd positioned myself close enough so she couldn't help but bump my arm as she moved away, I waited and prayed for a positive outcome.

Success! Lukewarm coffee splashed out of my still full cup, catching both of us exactly as I'd hoped.

"What the hell!"

My carefully rehearsed plan of campaign invoked the full force of Sheridan's wrath, and turned her hazel eyes to dark tortoiseshell in a split second. I couldn't have wished for a better result, now it all depended on her reaction to what came next.

"Oh dear, I am so sorry, Ms. Brooks." I dabbed ineffectually with an already soaked tissue at the dark stain spreading across the front of her shirt. The wet fabric clung like a second skin highlighting the swell of her breasts and rapidly hardening nipples. I licked my lips anticipating how they might feel in my mouth.

Maybe my tongue would do a better job of cleaning her up than this messy tissue.

"Stop! You're making it worse." She waved my hand away and pulled the edges of her jacket together to hide the stain.

Was that it? I'd counted on Sheridan offering more than this feeble reaction. My heart sank. *Had the sacrifice of my shirt been for nothing?*

While I was still bemoaning my plight, Sheridan flicked a brief glance around the room then drew herself up to her full height and fixed me with a steely glare. "Come!" Her commanding tone offered me no chance of refusal, even before her hand closed around my arm like a manacle. Her firm grasp left me no option but to keep pace with her when she frog-marched me from the conference room and along the corridor to the executive rest room.

She closed the door and clicked the lock into place before releasing her hold. I flexed the cramp out of my arm and concentrated on suppressing the bubble of near hysterical laughter that filled my throat. So far, my wild plan had worked like a charm but it was too early to celebrate the sort of victory I'd hoped to achieve.

Sheridan shrugged out of her jacket and then her shirt. I followed every movement with eager anticipation. When she bent over the sink to rinse the green silk under running water, the sight of her breasts encased in a flesh colored strapless lace bra that left little to the imagination sent my libido racing into overdrive. I bit down hard on my bottom lip to prevent myself propositioning her there and then like some cheap tart. My long-term plan needed much more finesse if it was to succeed.

After a moment, I pulled myself together and followed her lead casually removing my cotton top, as if it was something I did every day of the week. At which point I thanked the Good Lord that I never wore a bra. I moved to the sink and concentrated on sluicing the coffee stained fabric, using the mirror to keep tabs on Sheridan while she passed her shirt under the blast of hot air from the hand drier then held it up to the light.

"Damn! This is totally ruined." Sheridan tossed the shirt into the trash and glared at my reflection then her fiery gaze dipped lower. She stared long and hard at my naked tits. Under her scrutiny my nipples rose to the challenge, offering her an open invitation should she choose to take it, they peaked in tingling anticipation of the erotic pleasure her hands or lips might bring to bear. For what seemed endless seconds she remained impassive, then her tongue snaked out to moisten her lips. She reached out to circle one tight bud with a perfectly manicured fingernail, watching my reaction in the mirror. Her lips parted in a sensuous smile then, unexpectedly, she raked the blood-red varnished talon across the sensitized tip.

My body answered with a rush of liquid heat that pooled between my thighs and I was powerless to hold back the sharp intake of breath that betrayed my arousal. I dropped my top into the sink and squeezed my thighs together to trap the fire that licked at my throbbing pussy before I turned to face her.

"So, little girl…You fancy me, do you?"

"I'm not a—"

"Little girl." Sheridan chopped off my protest, her barbed sarcasm cutting like a sharp scalpel through soft flesh.

Too right. I definitely considered myself a woman. An experienced one too, since I could boast a string of well-satisfied lovers over recent years, and at thirty-one, was two years older than the twenty-nine stated in her bio. I even matched her for height at around five foot eight. Although I could never lay claim to her innate poise or elegance.

A smile played at the corner of her mouth. "So what do I call you?"

"Ria." I couldn't believe we'd almost got it on together and she didn't even know my name. Although why would she? The agency employed over five hundred people worldwide, it'd be nigh on impossible for her to put names to the faces of each and every one in the short time she'd been with the company.

She raised a quizzical eyebrow. "Ria is short for what?"

"Victoria... Victoria Bayliss."

"So, Ria, are you playing a dangerous game of dare with me, or do you really want me to fuck you?"

Her gaze held me captive, poised on the edge of a precipice. My body screamed for her touch yet something held me back from taking the final step. I couldn't blame my hesitation on her seniority or the fact we were in a work environment, which had never bothered me in the past. I suppose I just wasn't used to somebody else making all the running.

I exhaled slowly and eased closer. "Yes." Maybe the act of unbridled sex would release the emotional tension coiled in my system and allow me to think rationally.

Sheridan mirrored my movement. Her advance forced me backward until she'd trapped my body against the counter that divided the sinks. Then she dipped her head to capture my lips. I opened them on her command and the pungent tang of menthol enlivened the inside of my mouth as our tongues intertwined fighting for supremacy, a battle she won. Her searing kiss proved a catalyst. I lost control. A dam burst deep inside me, allowing waves of sensation to rocket through my body making everything I'd experienced in the past seem tame by comparison. If she could perform this magic with just a kiss then I wanted more. My heart hammered fit to burst as I battled for control of my body and my mind.

Before I realized her intention, she'd unzipped my jeans and pushed them down until they fell around my ankles then she thrust one hand between my thighs. I struggled to contain my composure when her fingers eased my cotton briefs aside and dipped into my wetness. At that moment, I wanted her more than I'd ever wanted anybody in my whole life.

My hands roamed freely over her exposed skin, it felt like silk under my touch and each sweep of my fingers wafted a warm floral perfume into the mix of our musky sexual need. I felt for the fastening on her bra and slipped the hook free allowing the scrap of silk to fall to the floor leaving her generous breasts unfettered ready for my delight. I wasted no time cupping their weight, using my thumbs to tease the nipples into hard buds. After a few minutes, her body tensed and shuddered. Then, without warning, she withdrew her lips from mine, and her fingers from my pussy, leaving me in breathless disarray and wondering where we went from here.

My tangled emotions didn't allow for rational thought, on one hand I wanted more from her than just a quickie in the rest room—much more, but right now I didn't care about the future. I needed her so badly the pain tore at every nerve ending.

While I was still dithering, Sheridan took charge of the situation and lifted me up onto the counter. I kicked my shoes and jeans clear of my feet as she moved in for the kill. Her lips trailed hot kisses down my throat, skimmed along my collarbone, and then traveled lower until she reached my breasts.

Her breath on my ultra-sensitive skin prompted an erotic tingle to fizz through my body like an electric charge and almost catapulted me into orbit. I grabbed a handful of her hair and held on tight while she took me on an incredible roller coaster ride, courtesy of her lips, teeth, and tongue.

Just when I thought things couldn't get any better, Sheridan placed her hands behind my ass and eased me forward until I was poised on the edge of the counter. It took a simple flick of her wrist to rip the cheap cotton briefs clear of my body before she pushed my thighs apart. I swallowed a gasp when cool air kissed my moist heat. My breathing caught and almost stopped like somebody or something had sucked all the air out of my lungs. Her hand slid between my thighs and I nearly climaxed at the first touch of her fingers on my clit. She moved sensuously, back and forth, first teasing the hard nub then deviating to replenish the moisture from my juices.

Jeez! If I didn't come soon I'd explode. I moaned aloud.

Sheridan must have sensed my urgency. She stepped back and reached for the zipper on her skirt. It slithered to the floor around her feet and a flesh-colored strap-on sprang to life. It jutted so proudly from its harness that I could almost imagine it real and pulsing with energy.

"Fuck me!" I voiced my astonishment that she'd managed to conceal that life-like dildo under her clothes all this time.

Did she wear it to work every day?

Was she in the habit of having sex with colleagues in the restroom?

The questions were irrelevant. I needed to feel that potent force deep inside me, pumping me dry and draining me of this unbearable tension. My internal muscles contracted in feverish anticipation of our coming together.

"It'll be my pleasure." Sheridan grinned and then with barely a pause for breath surged forward.

I took the full length inside me, my eager pussy welcoming the velvet-soft shaft with a firm grasp. She began to move with long slow stokes, almost withdrawing then plunging deep, the silicone beast moving freely in my slick hole. Her hot breath fanned my neck as she nibbled at the soft flesh of my throat. I splayed my hands on the counter behind me for support, wrapped my legs around her waist and tried to force the pace but she resisted my urging. Her hands crept between us to caress my breasts, before rolling the hard nipples between her fingers. My muscles spasmed around the hard dildo but still she didn't up the pace.

"Please…I need to come." I pushed my pelvis forward and tightened my legs around her waist seeking deeper penetration. Eventually she got the message and began to move faster, her stroke shortening to compensate.

As Sheridan approached her own climax, she used the full force of her nails to pinch my taut nipples. I threw my head back and met her thrust for thrust, our bodies working in unison, we rushed toward that special state of being where time and place have no existence and life dissolves into total oblivion.

My screams echoed off the tiled walls totally drowning out the sound of Sheridan's ragged gasps. With a final shudder, she fell on top of me, pushing me hard back against the mirror.

We remained locked together, motionless, for several seconds. The sound of our labored breathing so loud it drowned out the hum of the air-conditioning. Sheridan recovered first sliding off me she moved to the far sink and released the dildo from its flesh-colored harness. She took her time meticulously washing the shaft then using a wad of tissues to dry it thoroughly before reattaching it to the harness. Once Sheridan had dressed, I hardly noticed she wasn't wearing a shirt. The bra and jacket combination gave her an amazingly deep, sexy, cleavage. Engrossed in dreams of the future, it took me a while to realize that she'd cleaned herself up and dressed all without a single word or even the briefest of glances in my direction.

Tears misted my vision as realization dawned. Now she'd had her fun Sheridan clearly had no further use for me. With a heavy heart, I slid off the counter, gathered up my jeans and shoes then slipped into them both in seconds. My ruined briefs joined Sheridan's shirt in the trash before I rescued my top from the sink. The hot air hand drier made short work of drying the wet patch although there were still several dark splodges from the coffee, which would probably never wash out. However, the stains would add verisimilitude to any explanation I might need to make to cover the prolonged absence from my desk, assuming anyone had even noticed the empty chair. My watch confirmed barely thirty minutes had elapsed since the meeting finished.

I slipped the top over my head and then glanced in the mirror to check how disheveled I looked. Ugh! My hair, never very tidy at the best of times, resembled a bird's nest. I combed my fingers through the unruly curls only to discover, when I pushed the hank of hair away from my face that Sheridan had sucked at my neck in her moment of passion.

Hell and damnation! That prominent red mark was a dead giveaway to what I'd been up to in the past half hour, but I'd have to brazen it out since there was no possibility I'd have a tube of concealer in my purse, I never used much in the way of make-up at the best of times and none for work.

After giving my reflection a final check, I turned and found Sheridan waiting by the door clearly impatient for me to leave. An icy frisson trickled down my spine when I clashed with her uncompromising gaze and any thoughts of trying to make further contact vanished in an instant. I refused to beg and give her the satisfaction of snubbing me. Instead, I took a deep breath and with as much poise as I could muster given the circumstances, walked right past her with head held high.

Not wanting to meet anybody or face potentially awkward questions as to what I was doing up here, I took the fire stairs down to my workstation on the second floor.

How could my instinct have been so wrong about Sheridan Brooks?

The cold bitch had stolen my heart and I had to find a way to get it back.

I don't know how I got through the rest of the day. Despite my good intentions to forget she existed, I had difficulty in dismissing Sheridan, or our activities in the restroom, from my mind. Images of her frigid demeanor haunted me, playing over and over like some grotesque video at the back of my eyes. Several times I was tempted to drop everything, rush upstairs to her office, grab her then put her across my knee and spank the ice-queen bitch out of her until she begged me to fuck her.

With less than half an hour to go before the end of the day, I received an email message from my line manager to report immediately to Karen Lucas of human resources. This unusual occurrence niggled at my stomach all the way up to her fifth floor office. I remembered Karen, from my job interview two years ago, as a pleasant motherly type, somebody I wouldn't normally have worried about facing. However, if Sheridan Brooks was behind this summons then the call upstairs took on a new and completely sinister meaning the consequences of which didn't bear thinking about.

I certainly owed thanks to whichever guardian angel had prompted me to miss lunch in favor of some essential clothes shopping. I'd certainly feel much less at a disadvantage facing up to whatever awaited me wearing a smart new top with a high neck and fresh underwear.

Karen, who had the grace to look somewhat uncomfortable as she welcomed me into her office and invited me to take a seat, soon confirmed my fears. She skirted around the subject for something like five minutes before getting to the point. I actually began to feel quite sorry for the poor woman, forced into a situation for which she clearly had no heart. Apparently, due to the recession, the agency had to cut back on staff. A draw had taken place of staff eligible for immediate redundancy and my name came out first. I didn't believe a word of this spiel, coming on top of my sex session with the ice queen but I let Karen go through the motions without comment. The redundancy package on offer was extremely generous, better than I could have hope for considering my short service.

Clearly, Sheridan Brooks was prepared to pay big money to get rid of me without delay. Presumably, to guard against of any possible embarrassment that may follow from our brief liaison.

Did she worry I'd broadcast details of our casual fuck in the restroom all over the agency?

I wanted to laugh but Karen would have thought me totally crazy. Instead, I put on a solemn expression and enquired about a testimonial and if I must work out my notice.

Surprise, surprise, Karen confirmed my employment here would cease as soon as I signed the acceptance of terms she handed me.

I signed. Karen assured me the promised settlement would follow within a few days. Then she shook my hand and wished me luck before handing me an envelope containing a copy of the contract and a glowing reference she was confident would help me find a fabulous new job in days. Where this new post was going to come from in the current climate defied imagination.

* * * *

The following month passed in a whirl of job applications matched by either total silence or if I was really lucky a rejection letter. I did a daily round of the recruitment agencies and sent my résumé to several online sites too with little or no response. When I got home each evening, even my apartment gave me no solace. The soft lights and soothing color scheme made me restless for company. I hadn't had a regular lover for ten months, since Clara's promotion and subsequent posting to Hong Kong. At first we'd kept in touch by Skype and IM then, inevitably, she met somebody else and our contact ceased. Over the past few months, I'd been quite content alone, venturing out occasionally to meet up with friends for drinks or a meal. Now I positively craved Sheridan's company. The wanting tortured me, until I felt like a dehydrated woman denied the thirst-quenching water placed just out of her reach. The one woman I couldn't have and didn't want at any price invaded my entire existence with her presence. I tried in vain to convince myself that she no longer existed and could rot in hell as far as

I was concerned. Yet for some inexplicable reason, none of my attempts to dismiss her from my head or my heart worked.

Everything I did seemed to conjure up her image, even here in my apartment where she'd never been. I pictured us, sharing a drink, a meal, or snuggled together on the sofa watching TV and worst of all making love all through the night. Every time her image filled my vision, the need surged through my body leaving me over-heated, wet, breathless and ready to scream.

My obsession with Sheridan Brooks took a more serious turn when I found myself taking a deliberate detour past the agency building one evening in the hope of catching a glimpse of her. Then I knew it was time to take action before things got really out of hand and I became a stalker.

The lease on my apartment had barely two months left to run so I took that as an omen to move away— right away from Sheridan, to another city. Much as I hated to leave New York, with no job and no prospect of finding one unless I worked night shift stacking supermarket shelves or cleaning offices, a change of scene made perfect sense. Thanks to the generous payoff, I had plenty of money in the bank and the free time to make a leisurely transition between cities.

Boston called me home, especially as I could stay with my cousin for a month or two while I attempted to carve out a new career for myself and found somewhere to put down new roots. The advertising world being relatively small and close knit I didn't fancy my chances if I stayed on this career path. Sooner or later I'd come up against Sheridan and be forced into retreat once again.

Two weeks into my preparations, I paid a flying visit to Lynnette in Boston taking some things that weren't going into storage. We spent Saturday together getting my room sorted out then I caught up with old friends over Sunday brunch before I took the train back to New York and my now very bare apartment.

My heart sank when I discovered Sheridan had called in my absence. Not once, not twice, but six clipped messages waited on my answering machine. Her messages offered no clue as to what or why, just her name, the time, and that she'd call back—I didn't want her to. She'd blown her chances by her callous behavior. I never wanted to speak to her again.

Yet perversely, my curiosity piqued, I longed for her to call again so I could find out what had been worth six calls.

Why had she bothered to contact me now, after all this time?

What was so important?

The telephone remained stubbornly silent through several long days and nights while I continued my packing. By the weekend, I reached the conclusion that Sheridan had thankfully given up on whatever plan she'd devised to fuck with my life for a second time.

Saturday lunchtime saw me heading for the Heartland Brewery on Fifth Avenue for the regular monthly get together with several old college friends, which turned into an impromptu farewell party for me. Our lunch date stretched into the late afternoon with many toasts and much hilarity, the result no doubt of freely flowing quantities of our favorite Summertime Apricot and Indian River Light Ales. When I staggered home to Harlem burdened under the weight of many farewell gifts, I found Sheridan waiting on the doorstep of my building.

I hardly recognized her. Dressed casually in a nondescript gray hooded sweatshirt, matching sweat pants and trainers she looked no different from the army of joggers who frequent the running track around Central Park at this time of year. By the time, I realized her identity it was far too late to turn tail and run even had I been capable of such a feat. Instead, I stood and stared like an idiot while my heartbeat accelerated into overdrive.

"Ria…you are here." Sheridan met my vacant gaze with a smile that made me think of a cat with a bowl of cream. "I thought I'd missed you yet again."

Somehow, I managed to control the urge to throw myself into her arms, to force my befuddled brain to ignore her overture and the insistent throbbing in my crotch. It took all my concentration to step around her and swipe my key card to unlock the outer door and wedge it open with my hip. Unfortunately, I hadn't accounted for the packages, which spilled from my arms and landed at our feet on the top step. We both bent down at the same time and almost bumped heads. I reached for my scattered gifts but only managed to grab two of the brightly decorated bags while Sheridan outwitted me and snagged most of them. She stood up, clutching her spoils, leaving me at a distinct disadvantage and moved swiftly past me into the lobby.

I followed more slowly. The outer door closed behind me with loud bang like a prison cell door trapping us together in the small foyer.

Fearing the worst if she got any closer, I held my hands out for the packages. "I can manage now."

Sheridan fixed me with a long, hard, stare and shook her head. "Allow me to help you up to your apartment." Without waiting for my response, she pressed the elevator call button.

No! Don't let her do this.

Too late my brain accelerated into action and screamed for me to stop Sheridan, that it was a bad idea to allow her back into my life even for a second. However, by the time I gathered my scattered wits we were inside the elevator and already heading up.

Why wasn't I surprised that she knew which floor to select?

Sharing this confined space with Sheridan gave me goose bumps. On the one hand, I desperately wanted to pin her up against the wall and fuck the uppity bitch out of her. While on the other hand, my sense of self-preservation told me I needed to keep as much distance between us as possible.

The elevator jolted to a halt, and the whoosh of air as the door opened matched my sigh of relief. Once again, Sheridan took the lead leaving me trailing in her wake.

How did she know to turn left when we exited the elevator?

Deep in thought, I shadowed her along the fifth floor hallway towards my door, wondering how I was going to get inside without Sheridan assuming she had an open invitation to tag along.

I didn't make it.

Sheridan followed me into the lounge and added her contribution to the two gift bags I tossed haphazardly onto the table. Her glance flitted around the room, now stripped bare of everything bar the basic furniture that came with the apartment then back to me a deep frown creasing her brow.

"Have you adopted a minimalist lifestyle?"

Beyond words, I shook my head, unexpectedly close to tears. A lump like a gigantic football formed in my throat and made speech nigh on impossible. She looked so right here in my lounge, just as I'd imagined her in all the fantasies that had played through my mind over the past weeks. Yet I knew her presence could only bring me abject misery. Much as I loved Sheridan, there was little chance of a future for us or even of her reciprocating my love. She didn't see me in that way — truth to tell, I didn't know how she saw me or what she hoped to achieve by coming here but whatever her plan I had no doubt it would plunge me deeper into the pit of unbearable pain and unhappiness.

Suddenly the room became unstable, heaving and rocking like the uncontrolled movement of a violent earthquake. I blinked rapidly, trying hard to focus on Sheridan's gorgeous face but everything dissolved into a swirling gray mist. Then I was falling, spinning in space, as if I'd stepped out of my body into a vortex. I fought against the force sucking me into oblivion, trying desperately to cling onto reality yet losing the battle.

"Ria!" I didn't recognize the alien voice calling my name. "Wake up. Please." Someone gripped my shoulder and shook me hard. I tried to open my eyes to see who was giving me grief but my body failed to respond.

Firm hands grasped me and lifted me up. A clean aroma, of delicately perfumed soap wafted in the air and caressed my senses. I relaxed, feeling incredibly secure, and safe, cradled against a warm female chest.

"Please wake up. Ria, darling, I can't stand to see you like this."

Like what?

Darling?

What's going on?

Where am I and who is this person?

Nothing made sense until my eyes finally opened to reveal Sheridan's face in close-up a worried frown creasing her brow.

"Thank goodness!" Her face cleared. "I thought I'd lost you."

Lost me? I shook my head, more to clear my brain than in response to her statement. Although on that point she'd never had me, in the sense of us being an item, a couple. A brief, though enjoyable, fuck in a restroom didn't count in my book. With my chest pressed against hers, my body tuned into the rhythmic beat of her heart, the fast pulse matched my own. Warmth spread through my body converging at my core. I snuggled closer driven by an irresistible desire to reinforce our connection, to make sure this wasn't another fantasy. The need touch her, kiss her, to bury my face in her tits, take her to my bed and fuck her non-stop until the sun came up, overwhelmed me.

Hell! Where was my common sense? Had her second intrusion into my life robbed me of all vestiges of reason? I had to distance myself from temptation, and get her out of my orbit fast, before I said or did, something I'd regret for the rest of my life. I struggled free of her arms, staggered across the room on legs that felt like rubber and flopped onto the window seat.

Sheridan followed, stopping a few feet away from me by the table. She idly fingered one of the shiny pink gift bags then gave me a puzzled look. "I thought you birthday was in October."

Was there anything Sheridan didn't know about me?

"It is." I broke eye contact reluctant to divulge the reason behind the gifts. The less she knew about my impending move to Boston the better. In less than forty-eight hours, I'd be gone for good, saying a sad farewell to all my dreams, to New York, and Sheridan. The last thing I needed now was any interference or I might be tempted to change my mind.

Sheridan huffed, clearly dissatisfied with my noncommittal response. When she realized nothing more was forthcoming from me, she opened one of the bags and pulled out a card. Even from a distance, the large bright pink letters scrawled across the design jumped right off the page and hit me between the eyes, the message was impossible to miss— Goodbye!

"You're leaving?" She studied the card then turned her attention to me, her frown deepening. "Going where?" Disbelief dripped from her voice.

I shook my head. My stomach knotted painfully and nausea burned my throat. The thought of never seeing her again tortured me yet I knew it was the only way to preserve my sanity.

"When?" Sheridan's glare drilled into me. "Answer me, damn you."

Her anger puzzled me. "Why should I?" I shrugged my shoulders. "What I do is none of your business." How she had the nerve to come here and start questioning my decisions was beyond comprehension.

Sheridan advanced toward me. "I'm making it my business." She stopped inches from my seat, towering over me, and used one finger to tip my chin up forcing me to make eye contact. "You can't leave me now. I won't let you go."

I expelled my tension on a ragged breath. "You can't stop me. I've given up this apartment, made all the arrangements, and—"

"Then cancel them. I want you to stay."

Much as it moved me, I resisted Sheridan's passionate plea. On past performance, she didn't have the right to demand anything of me. "No way!"

"Please! I've gone out on a limb to keep you in my life."

Now it was my turn to frown. "Really?" From my perspective, she'd done the exact opposite. "I'd love to hear you explain how getting paid off without notice was designed to keep me in your life?"

"It was." Sheridan sighed. "I had to do it, to protect you from the fall-out."

"What fall-out? You're not making any sense."

"You must know that the agency has a strict policy of no workplace liaisons, even between the heterosexual staff. Alvin D Klingman, the firm's founder, who believed in a strict moral code of behavior, wrote it into the original employment contract way back in the 1930's and its remained in place right through to the present day. Imagine the directorial furor when our little tryst came to light courtesy of a nosy junior exec with her eye on promotion. I had to get you out of there before the shit hit the proverbial fan."

"I still don't see the logic here. You kept your job but I had to go...A bit one-sided wouldn't you say?"

Sheridan's laughter echoed around the near empty apartment. "I'm not employed there any more either. I resigned the same day, immediately after I sorted out your redundancy package. In case you're wondering I put up the severance money myself and enlisted Karen's help to make everything appear above board."

Her explanation sounded too fantastic for words. "Why should I trust anything you say?" Did she think I was born yesterday? Even if what she said held true that still didn't explain her ice-queen performance or seven weeks silence—no, six if I took last weekend's calls into account.

Sheridan slid onto the window seat beside me and reached for my hand. "Because it's the truth. I've no reason to lie to you of all people. And before you ask, I started back at my old firm last week. It's quite a relief to be in a relaxed atmosphere again."

I snatched my hand out her grasp. "Okay. Assuming I accept your story, it still doesn't explain why you treated me with such icy contempt or kept silent for six weeks."

Her deep sigh disturbed the wind chime above our heads. Sheridan looked me in the eye. "I had my reasons. Mainly though, I needed time to think, to get to grips with the situation and see if the strange thoughts messing with my head were transitory or something more permanent. At first, I didn't dare to believe that I'd fallen in love for the first time in my life and with a complete stranger. Now I'm sure, so sure, I can say it aloud…I love you, Ria. I want to spend the rest of my life with you."

My heart almost stopped beating. Sheridan loved me! I shook my head, unable take in the enormity of her words.

She grinned. "Yes, I know, it sounds totally ridiculous when we've hardly spent any time together but I fell for you on sight the second you walked into that conference room. You have no idea how I suffered trying not to look at you while I finished my talk." Her impenetrable gaze bored into me just as it had on the morning we met. "I couldn't believe my luck when we accidentally bumped into each other."

"That was no accident."

"Really!" Her eyes widened. "You mean you…"

I nodded. "It seemed the only way to get your attention."

"Oh!" She looked totally bemused by my revelation.

Wait! Something still bothered me. "If everything you say is true, why were you wearing a strap-on to the office?"

"Would you believe to give me confidence? Sheridan shook her head. "No, I don't suppose you'd understand where I'm coming from unless I explain. It's no fun being the only woman, and a lesbian at that, in a male dominated environment. Wearing a dick under my clothes boosts my self-esteem and puts me on a level with them. Although until that day, I'd never used it in anger so to speak." Her lips quirked in a half smile. "Okay, I'll freely admit that I'd fantasized about doing so but never found the right opportunity or the right person. You were the first. How could I resist when you stripped off in front of me and flaunted those ripe tits in my face. You are one sexy lady."

Wow!

My heart swelled fit to burst out of my chest.

Sheridan thought me a sexy lady.

Never in a million years had that scenario crossed my mind. What a pity our affair petered out before it even really began. I wanted to show her just how sexy I could be if give free rein. Much as I'd wish for a happy ending. Or at best, a few weeks of sex, sex, and more sex until we'd satisfied every last vestige of our hunger I couldn't see any way forward.

"We have a lot of catching up to do." Sheridan flashed me a wicked smile. "I can't wait to get you naked and fuck your brains out."

She must be a mind reader. I returned her smile. "The feeling is mutual but..."

Sheridan trailed her fingers across my knee. "You surely can't deny we're good together."

A delightful shiver rippled through me and moist heat filled my pussy. "That's one point I won't argue."

"No point in wasting valuable time then." She circled the soft flesh half way up my thigh. "We'll be so good together."

How could I resist? Sheridan's arguments proved too persuasive. I smiled then leaned across to capture her lips with mine. Her mouth opened to my urging and my tongue plundered the moist depths. She tasted so good, sweet, chocolaty with a hint of vanilla and strawberry.

Sheridan met me half way, eager, hot, and oh so sexy. Suddenly, kissing wasn't enough to satisfy our need, we tore at clothes, at each other, with a frantic urgency to get maximum skin on skin contact. Finally, we ended up naked, on the floor in a tangle of arms and legs, breathless and laughing.

Determined to establish control I rolled Sheridan under me, pinned her to the wood and nestled my body between her open thighs. Our bodies fitted together in perfect harmony, breasts caressed breasts, silky soft shaven mounds pressed tight against each other. Sheridan ran her fingers lightly up my thighs sending glorious tingling sensations rippling through me. I kissed my way down her throat. Her skin felt like satin to my touch. A delicate perfume permeated the air around us. I moved lower to take one succulent nipple between my lips and tease it with my tongue.

Sheridan thrust her body toward me and raked her fingernails across my shoulders. "Oh, yes! More please..."

Her gasped entreaty spurred me on. I moved my mouth to her other breast, while manipulating the now wet nipple between thumb and forefinger. Already hard, it grew harder under my ministration.

Eager for maximum contact, I shifted my position until I could straddle one thigh and grind my clit against her soft flesh. My free hand sought her slit. Like me, she was soaking wet. When I slicked my fingers into her juices and teased her swollen clitoris, she moaned softly her breathing ratcheting up several notches.

"Fuck me. Please!" Her body moved under me and exquisite sensations raced to my core.

My fingers sought her slick hole. I used one finger to penetrate the moist depths then almost withdrew before thrusting deep again. She was so ready for me. I inserted a second finger, using my thumb to massage her engorged clit with each thrust and my fingertips to seek out her g-spot with each withdrawal. Sheridan was getting close, her pussy clenched around my hand and her increasingly frantic body movements matched my thrusts. Finally, I added a third finger, plunging faster, deeper, and harder.

She shuddered. "I can't hold on…I'm…" Her ragged pants urged me on.

Yes, I knew exactly how she felt. Our slick bodies moved in unison. Every reciprocal movement brought my ultra-sensitive clit into contact with her skin. The butch in me wanted to hold back, to satisfy my lady first but my body had other ideas. Driven on by my desire for release I moved faster, slamming against her, until I barely had control over my own raging climax let alone hers. Hot come flooded her thigh, slicking her skin, increasing the amazing potency of my orgasm. I grazed her nipple with my teeth, as glorious sensations continued to grip my body. When I felt her control begin to shatter, I immediately lifted my mouth from her breast, needing to witness her pleasure as I took her over the edge into free-fall, wanting to fix the moment in my memory for all time.

In the throes of her orgasm, Sheridan radiated incredible beauty, her lips parted and her hazel eyes morphed into deep, dark, pools of desire. I continued pumping deep inside her, prolonging her climax until she stopped gyrating and relaxed on a sigh. Tears formed in her eyes and overflowed from the corners.

Overcome with love, I leant forward to lap the moisture from her temple. Whatever the future held we would have this one precious moment to remember. Then I kissed her eyes her cheeks and finally her sweet lips, they parted, welcoming me inside. Our gentle, intimate, post-climactic kisses carried both emotion, and sadness.

How could I bear to leave her now?

Our sexual romp hadn't solved anything in fact it had made my situation worse. I pulled away from her and sat up, unable to share this cozy intimacy any longer.

"What's wrong?" Sheridan reached for me a frown creasing her brow.

"I'm sorry." I moved out of her orbit and grabbed for my clothes. "This isn't going to work. I think you should leave now."

"No!" Sheridan stamped a metaphorical foot. "We can make this work but you have to at least try to meet me half way."

A ragged sigh escaped my lips. "We can't, it's too late. I'd like nothing better than to take you to my bed and keep you there forever but I don't see how. By ten o'clock on Monday morning, I'll be gone from this apartment—and from New York for good." Nakedness was not a suitable state in which to debate this subject. I slipped my arms into my shirt, did up a few buttons and put some distance between us.

Sheridan stood but seemingly not bothered by her naked state made no attempt to dress herself. "Nonsense! You could stay if you really wanted to."

"How?" I shook my head and scrambled into my jeans. "It's too late to change my arrangements now. I'd need a place to stay for a start." If only we could turn back the clock but it was past time for regrets.

"Why not move in with me." She paced across the room to my side. "My apartment is plenty big enough for two."

She had an answer for everything but I didn't fancy being a kept woman. I shook my head. "Without a job I can't afford my share of the bills, and finding one is proving a bit of a problem. That's why I was going home."

Sheridan's glare sizzled, hot, like a branding iron straight out of the fire. "I'm not into long distance relationships. If I can't persuade you to stay in New York, you'll force me to follow you to wherever home is."

Was she serious?

Would she really follow me to the ends of the earth?

My surprise that Sheridan didn't already know about Boston, since she seemed to know everything else about me, overshadowed by her apparent determination to make our relationship work whatever the cost. I blinked back stinging tears of frustration.

Could I stay in New York—with her?

I struggled with such a momentous decision.

What did we really know about each other apart from our sexual compatibility?

Would a relationship between unequal partners really work?

Could I take a chance on love conquering all?

All the possible scenarios raced through my mind at breakneck speed resulting in a jumbled mess that resembled the aftermath of a car smash. Panic tied my stomach in knots and my heart thumped in my chest. It took an enormous effort to concentrate on steadying my breathing until the palpitations subsided.

"What do you say? Sheridan fixed me with a steady gaze. Will you stay with me?"

All my objections seemed superfluous when it came to the crunch, my need to be with her overshadowed everything in the whole world. I nodded. "I think we might give it a shot if you're sure, but I must pay my way."

Her face lit up in a smile. "Great! First, we need to get you moved before you change your mind. We can worry about the minor points later." She grabbed her sweat pants, pulled them on, not bothering with underwear, and followed up with the top then ran her fingers through her hair.

"Do you have to pack anything?" Sheridan glanced around at the shabby utility furniture and wrinkled her cute nose. "How much of this stuff yours?"

"The furniture all belongs to the apartment. I just have a few bags in the other room, everything else has gone into storage."

"Good! I'll call a cab while you get your things. I can't wait to get you settled in my apartment."

"You mean to go now—today?" Until she spoke, I hadn't considered the timing of any move outside the context of Monday being departure day.

"Why ever not?"

"Well, I don't know where to for a start. You never said where you stay or anything about the place and I need to let my family know about the change of arrangements."

"The Upper East Side—East 72nd. Sheridan glanced towards my single source of daylight—a small window affording the less than enticing view of a black-painted fire escape scrambling up the dirty gray-brown wall of the adjacent building. She turned back to me and grinned broadly. "After this, I'll guarantee you'll love my apartment and the views across Central Park."

My blood ran cold. I just knew there'd be a catch to mar my chance of happiness. "I can't afford to live there." My protest sounded lame, even to my ears, but it held the ring of truth. Always supposing I landed a fabulous new job tomorrow, a share in that area would be way above my budget and most probably my entire salary too.

Sheridan laughed and shook her head. "Of course you can. How much do you pay here?"

I bit my lip, reluctant to admit that what I paid each month probably wouldn't cover her service charges let alone the sky-high rent on a luxury apartment. Then I realized unless I told her the truth she couldn't possibly appreciate my predicament. "Eleven hundred a month plus utilities."

A frown creased her brow as she considered my statement. "How about eight hundred a month all inclusive?"

"Now you're insulting my intelligence." I turned away so she wouldn't see the tears of impotent rage filling my eyes. I hate being poor and hate it even more when people make special allowances for my impecunious state. She grabbed my arm and spun me around. "My offer is genuine. I want you to live with me and share my life."

Face to face with her angry glare, I had nowhere to hide. "I'm not a charity case." I wanted us to share too but not on her one-sided terms.

"I'm not treating you as one."

How could she claim that yet at the same time make such a temptingly low offer? I shook my head in bewilderment. A multitude of questions jostled for prominence yet none of them seemed remotely relevant given the circumstances. Fate had snatched away my chance to be with the woman I loved on an equal footing.

What else mattered?

"Then tell me how much rent you pay, plus the service charge and utilities." My request was more rhetorical, I didn't really expect her to respond.

"No problem." Sheridan shrugged. "Though I don't pay any rent, nor a mortgage, because I own the apartment outright. We just need to share the service charges and utilities. The exact figure escapes me right now but eight hundred will more than cover your share. That sum includes use of all the facilities including health club, pool, recreation room and roof deck."

Jeez!

Sheridan owned an apartment that probably carried a multi million-dollar price tag.

I couldn't decide if this revelation made things worse not better. "You must be very wealthy to own an apartment like that." My comment slipped out almost unbidden. To tell the truth, I had little idea how the other half lived, other than from the perspective of TV or the movies. Seems like I was about to find out first hand.

"Not so you'd notice." Sheridan smiled and shook her head. To put your mind at rest, I don't come from old money. I have to work, to live and pay my bills, like everybody else in these hard times. I inherited the apartment from my grandparents and they bought it when property was a lot less expensive than it is today."

Her explanation squashed all my objections. "If you're really sure about this then yes, I'll move in with you."

"In that case, what are we waiting for?"

"Nothing, I suppose…"

Sheridan grabbed me and swung me around in a wild dance, her whoop of joy echoing around the room. Then we collapsed in a heap, breathless and laughing, the battered sofa groaning under our joint weight.

I held her close and kissed her sweet lips, rejoicing our good fortune. We had love on our side and whatever the future held we'd face it together.

CONSUMING PASSION

I'd almost finished my shower when I caught the imperative summons of my cell phone above the rush of water.

What now?

My rage at the caller's lousy timing escaping in a rush of breath, I turned off the spray, grabbed a towel off the rail and wrapped it around my body sarong fashion then ran through to the bedroom to answer the summons.

"Hi Jay!" Arlene's breezy greeting soothed my irritation, replacing my angry scowl with a smile. "Um, sorry my dear, did I interrupt something?"

Her question took the sparkle out of my smile. "What makes you think that?" The towel chose that moment to slither down my body. I made a grab for it then tucked the end in more securely above my breasts.

"You sound out of breath like you've just had a fantastic orgasm." I heard the laughter in her voice and relaxed, admiring my new friend's directness. I'd only known Arlene for five days, since the previous Thursday to be precise, and already felt comfortable with her like we'd been friends all our lives. We'd got chatting while waiting at the Cape Air check-in at Logan airport. I'd arrived from New York and Arlene had been visiting her parents just outside Boston. We hadn't stopped talking for a second from then on until our shared cab dropped me off at my hotel. Provincetown during Women's Week is always a hive of activity. I liked to arrive a couple of days in advance to give myself time to acclimatize to the different pace of life and get into a relaxed frame of mind before the fun started.

"No such luck…I was just taking a shower."

"The perfect place for some people."

Arlene's easy assumption brought me up short. "Not for me." *At least not without a special somebody to share the experience.* My heart flipped as bitter memories tried to smash through the defensive barrier I'd built up. I shivered, feeling a sudden chill in the air then glanced down at the water pooling around my feet. "Did you want me for something important?"

"Yeah! I'm preparing supper and as usual I've made way too much for one so I wondered if you'd care to come over to help me eat it."

"Supper sounds great. Give me directions and I'll be right there." After a busy day rushing between meetings and several readings then to a late afternoon book signing, I relished the prospect of relaxing in pleasant company away from the crowds and away from—. No! I cut off that train of thought abruptly. "Can I bring anything?"

"Just yourself…and your appetite."

Did I detect a hint of innuendo?

No, I smiled and shook my head, more like my imagination working overtime. After spending the entire afternoon listening to a succession of erotic excerpts that left one panting for more it was no wonder I felt horny. Before I had time to pursue my thoughts further, Arlene continued speaking. "I'm in the west end of town." She rattled off the address and directions then added. "Don't be too long, the food's nearly ready."

Unlike me, Arlene is a permanent resident of Provincetown, she runs a jewelry business from a tiny store close to MacMillan Wharf. While I'm one of those transient visitors who fill the small coastal town to bursting point for one week each October. This year though, for the first time in six years, I'd come alone. Carrie, my long time girlfriend and muse, had deserted me for someone new. They'd met in Ptown last October and by early November. Carrie had packed up her belongings and left our Brooklyn apartment to shack up with her new lover in Norfolk, Virginia. I'd heard from friends they were in town this week and had purposely avoided all our old haunts. I didn't want to witness them fawning over each other like a couple of randy teens or, worse still, for them to see me alone and still feeling the raw pain of Carrie's betrayal with every breath I took.

I finished drying myself then quickly donned fresh underwear, jeans, and a loose-knit brown top over a cream shirt. A quick blast with the hairdryer left my casually styled short hair looking reasonably tidy, not that it mattered, I wasn't out to impress anybody. Within ten minutes of ending the call, I was out of my hotel and striding briskly along Commercial Street through the early evening crowds.

Even though Arlene had said not to bring anything, I couldn't resist buying her a box of chocolates—I already knew she had a passion for a particular brand—and a small posy of delicately scented freesias. Then, as an afterthought, I stopped off at the liquor store near her home for a bottle of my favorite wine—a fruity Californian Shiraz.

Arlene's narrow two-storey house was exactly where she'd described it, tucked away in a small courtyard at the far end of Tremont Street. I received an instant response to my knock, so quick in fact that she must have been waiting with her hand on the handle since she couldn't possibly see my approach from inside. She greeted me with a wide smile of welcome. My own smile morphed into open-mouthed surprise at the vision before me. I'd sort of got used to seeing my new friend in casual attire, jeans, a sweater and boots, with her hair in braids or at best twirled into an easy knot. Tonight, high-heeled sandals added several inches to her height raising her petite frame closer to my level. Shining blond waves tumbled about the shoulders of a fabulous midnight blue halter-neck tunic, worn over matching lace leggings. The plunging neckline offered a tantalizing view of a deep cleavage and the soft flowing material shot through with a silver thread design had transformed the woman I'd got to know into the most gorgeous femme.

"Jay! It's so good to see you again." Arlene hugged me with her natural enthusiasm and kissed me on both cheeks then finally brushed her lips across mine so briefly I couldn't decide if she'd intended the kiss or just caught my lips by mistake. She smelt as good as she looked. A soft yet irresistible fragrance enveloped my senses and carried me away into the realms fantasy.

Not wanting to explore that place just yet, I pulled myself together and offered her the flowers. "I know you said not to bring anything but I couldn't resist these."

"You are so bad." Arlene laughed as she raised the cellophane wrapped posy to her nose. "How did you know freesias are my favorites?" Then she leaned forward and sealed her mouth to mine in a way that left no room for error. Her velvet soft lips set my heart racing out of control and heat flooding to my core.

Jeez! I wasn't ready for this, for a new relationship, for casual sex even. My instinct hovered towards flight but something akin to a sense of, *OMG! I feel so fucking good*, kept my feet rooted to the spot.

To give myself a moment to recover from the dizzy spell brought on by her kiss, I produced both chocolates and wine from my bag. "Or these too...I hope you approve my choice of wine."

Arlene took the gifts with a shake of her head. "Bad, bad, girl, I shall have to find a way to punish you," she scolded, although the twinkle in her eyes said how much she appreciated what I'd brought. She glanced at the label. "Yes, I love this particular wine, but can we save it for another night since I already have champagne on ice for tonight?"

Never one to turn down champagne, I nodded, smiling at the unexpected vision of where all those sexy bubbles might lead us. "No problem." I liked her suggestion. The idea of us sharing the wine on some other occasion sounded cozy and gave our new friendship an air of semi-permanence.

A gorgeous savory aroma wafted through from the kitchen prompting a loud rumble from my stomach. "Sorry." I grinned and patted my midriff in apology. "I haven't eaten since breakfast and my stomach is protesting." That situation was not unusual. Never a big eater at the best of times, the substantial breakfast buffet served at my hotel each morning usually kept me going all day. By evening, though, I was more than ready to sample the colorful atmosphere and mouthwatering delights of Napi's or Bubala's by the Bay.

Arlene gave me a stern look and waggled her finger. "You should eat regular meals, it's not good to starve yourself all day. Come through to the lounge so we can rectify your sorry state immediately." She placed her gifts on the console table and tucked her arm into mine then led me further down the hall. The gentle strains of the adagio from Mozart's clarinet concerto grew louder as we rounded the corner and moved closer to a half open door. "In here." She pushed the door wide open then stood back to let me enter.

Candlelight bathed everything in a mellow glow like soft moonlight. "Oh, wow!" I stopped dead just inside the room, unable to believe my eyes. "This is amazing."

Yards of filmy midnight blue and silver fabric draped artistically over decorated wooden poles dressed the windows to perfection. A circular glass table mounted on a spectacular piece of bleached driftwood immediately captured my attention— being the only piece of furniture in the whole room probably had something to do with it. As the table stood barely eighteen inches off the floor, the seating logically comprised large cushions also covered in shades of blue and silver. A subtle vanilla perfume pervaded the air from the many scented candles set in decorative triple wall sconces. The whole effect reminded me of a Bedouin tent. Like the one I'd dined in many years ago whilst on a camel safari into the Sahara desert during a visit with friends to Tunisia.

I turned to witness Arlene's smile and the pleasure lighting up her beautiful amber eyes. "I'm really glad you like it. When I first moved to Ptown and bought the house I arranged it like this to save my money for the business but now I love it so much I don't want to change a thing."

My gaze locked with hers and the breath caught in my throat. "I'm not surprised. It's absolutely beautiful..." I almost added "like you" but stopped myself just in time. I didn't know her well enough yet to make comments of that nature. "...and so perfectly coordinated."

"Thank you." Arlene smiled broadly then dipped her head, a faint blush coloring her cheeks. "Please make yourself at home." The pressure of her hand in the small of my back as she urged me forward sent exciting tingles racing through my body. "I'll just put the flowers in water and get the rest of the food then we can eat."

Moving closer, I found the table already laden with a multitude of small dishes each containing a different food. All this for just two people? Something didn't add up but I couldn't put my finger on it. I shook my head in total amazement unable to accept that Arlene would go to so much trouble for herself or even the two of us. From cold meats and shellfish, to several different kinds of olives and capsicums, as well as other prepared vegetables, salads and pickles, some of which I couldn't identify. The addition of dips, breads and assorted dishes of fruit and other sweet things, with a few empty spaces that looked ready to receive something hot completed the spread. In the center of all this amazing food stood a burbling water feature.

I turned away from the table before I disgraced myself by prematurely picking at the feast and gave my attention to her artwork. Like the rest of the room, her pictures followed a theme, mainly abstracts a mixture of vibrant hues and pastel shades all swirled together into amazing fractals yet still retaining a recognizable image. In addition to the abstracts, something else caught my eye—the striking pen and ink study of a nude stood out by being completely different from all the other pictures.

Was it of Arlene?

Impossible to tell, with the head turned away although the artist had drawn every other feature of the seated figure with great attention to detail. I moistened my dry lips and let my eyes trace the erotic pose to the focal point between the model's thighs.

Did the flowing tunic Arlene wore hide this delectable frame?

I couldn't wait to find out. My body thrummed with the euphoric anticipation of sampling those generous tits or burying my face in that exquisitely inviting pussy.

Fuck!

What am I doing?

Before I recovered from the shock of finding myself contemplating sex with a woman I hardly knew, Arlene returned carrying three dishes with the skill of an experienced waitress. She placed them on the table then dropped easily onto a cushion. I willingly banished all the erotic thoughts from my mind, crossed the room and followed her lead.

"Will you do the honors?" Arlene passed me the bottle of champagne. I popped the cork and aimed the foaming wine at the two flutes she held ready. Seeing the white froth erupt from the narrow opening set my thoughts racing towards a spontaneous orgasm. Heat flooded to my core and my insides pulsed, hungry and impatient for action. I reached around her and returned the bottle to the ice bucket my arm brushing her bare shoulder. At that point, I could have done with an ice bath myself. Her proximity did things to my body I'd almost forgotten. She handed me one of the flutes, and we toasted each other then she took a sip of wine, meeting my gaze coquettishly over the rim of her glass. Arlene's sexy smile offered unimaginable delights if I chose to take up her offer.

Arlene broke eye contact then set her glass down. "Let's eat!" She pointed in turn to the recent arrivals.

"From right to left are spicy ribs, Thai fish cakes, and the skewers hold marinated chicken with satay sauce, all homemade." She handed me a plate, together with a pair of chopsticks and a narrow two-pronged fork wrapped in a napkin. "The rest I'm sure you can fathom out for yourself. Dig in!"

With hunger gnawing at my insides, I needed no further urging from this kitchen Goddess. While I always enjoyed eating good food, my cooking skills were limited to the basics. The chance to indulge my palate on this scale came about rarely.

We ate in silence for several minutes, each dipping into whatever took our fancy until I glanced over and caught Arlene watching me intently. Once she had my full attention, her deeply intense, alluring, expression held me captive while she speared a tiny Thai fish cake and dunked it into the bowl of dipping sauce, letting the excess drip off before lifting it close to her mouth. Her full red lips parted slightly then her tongue darted out to circle them in a sensuous gesture before, with a quick flick, it snared the succulent morsel and took it inside her mouth. Finally, she licked the juices off her lips and sighed. These deliberately provocative actions lit a fire in my belly. I wanted her to treat my clit with the same relish, to feel her tongue sweeping across my sensitive flesh, and to experience the exquisite delight of it doing wonderful things to my overheated body. My pussy immediately drenched in the moist heat of desire.

Suddenly all the clues clicked into place in my brain like finding the final piece in a jigsaw. Arlene had planned this whole evening, from the pseudo casual invitation, to the elaborate meal together with candlelight and soft music, specifically to seduce me into submission. Fool that I am I had fallen headlong into her trap, like an innocent lamb to the slaughter, and I felt totally stupid for not catching on sooner.

Why hadn't I seen it coming?

Had she done this before?

Was I just one in a long line of women she fucked using food as bait?

Did it matter?

No. I answered the last question first then dismissed the others as irrelevant. Her interest flattered me enormously. I felt uplifted by the attentions of a woman young and gorgeous enough to have first pick from Ptown's annual influx of lesbian visitors. More importantly, this was the first time in a whole year I'd felt anything resembling sexual interest in anyone. I didn't plan to allow the past to fuck up my chances, or neglect to follow this amazing opportunity through to wherever it led. I deserved a slice of happiness and with Arlene offering me the full cake including the icing I fully intended to dive in and sample every delightful crumb.

The butch in me wanted to seize control of the situation but something compelled me to hold back and take my cue from Arlene. To discover how far she was prepared to take this erotic seduction quest. Although provocative behavior was totally out of character for me, her sultry expression egged me on. I soon discarded my inbred inhibitions and joined in the game exhibiting reckless wantonness as each new food played across my tongue.

Arlene held me prisoner, trapped by her hypnotic sensuality while she used a large shrimp to tease the outline of her lips with all the eroticism and expertise of a porn star addressing a dildo. Her tongue curled sinuously around the soft pink flesh, savoring it with long sweeps, before drawing it into her mouth. She sighed and closed her eyes releasing me to dwell in my vivid imagination as I pictured her doing the same to my clit. My breathing ratcheted up a notch.

The longer we played this game of seduction the hotter, wetter, and more excited I became by an experience that offered infinite freedom of expression as well as the pleasure of consuming delectable food. Hunger and sexual desire are, in my mind, inextricably linked by a base need to both eat and fuck, with mouths and vaginas being similar organs whose sole purpose is stimulation and gratification. The texture of food or other objects we insert into those orifices tend to satisfy both kinds of hunger as well as heightening sexual awareness.

We continued our seductive game a while longer then Arlene suddenly changed the rules and upped the stakes. "Here, try this." She offered me a tidbit on the tip of her fork.

The intensity of her gaze deepened as I accepted the offering and her lips parted on a sigh of pleasure as if I'd just swept my tongue across her clit. My heart flipped. The intimacy of the moment sent a rush of warmth coursing through my veins. From that point on, we fed each other turn and turn about. Each vying for number one spot in our expressions of sensual delight yet needing no words to convey those erotic messages. The game continued getting more overtly sexual and more abandoned, until the succulent sliver of roasted red capsicum I offered Arlene dripped juices down her chin. I watched, fascinated, as the liquid traced her throat and disappeared down into her gorgeous cleavage.

Fuck! I couldn't stand any more of this erotic torture. I needed to take control. "Hey, Arlene. We don't want to mess up your lovely top." Without waiting for her response, I reached around and unfastened the halter-neck tie. The silky material slithered down her body to pool around her waist. She wasn't wearing a bra. Her breasts were perfect, firm and ripe with dark aureoles and prominent nipples that begged for my attention.

Smiling, I followed the trail of juice with one finger then raised the digit to her lips. They parted and she tasted the tip of my finger with her tongue before drawing it deep inside her mouth, she swept the full length from tip to base, sucking hard then swirling her tongue around it. The unbelievable sensation of Arlene feeding off my finger like it was my clit nearly brought me to a premature orgasm. I withdrew the digit very slowly, resisting the urge to snatch it away, ground my ass into the cushion and strove to clear my mind of lurid thoughts like using my tongue to explore where my finger had recently been. I wasn't successful.

Arlene sighed deeply then she reached for my hand and dipped my fingers into a dish of smooth guacamole. She placed my hand to her chest and moved it in a lazy circle. I focused on the smears of avocado mixture adorning her gorgeous tits and my mouth filled with saliva. I longed dive in and taste her. To take one of her nipples between my lips, to play it with my tongue, but I held back forcing myself to take things slowly and keep the tension building as long as possible. Using my thumbs, I spread the soft green paste over the tips feeling them harden and swell in response.

"Please, Jay." Arlene groaned and thrust her tits forward. I smiled at her eagerness and used one hand to scoop up some soft taramasalata, smoothing the new mixture into her skin, mingling pale green and pink in a delightful swirled design. "Oh...yes!" Encouraged by this response, I leant in and swept my tongue across her breast. The subtle mix of creamy avocado and fish delighted my taste buds while the sensation of her nipples sliding against my tongue sent throbbing heat cascading through my body. I took one pert nipple between my teeth and bit down gently but firmly. A shiver rippled through her body and transferred to me by magic. Delightful pulses of energy traveled swiftly to every nerve ending.

"Wait! Dammit!" Arlene reached for me, tugging at my clothes until I released her tit just long enough to allow her to slip my sweater over my head. She dealt with my shirt and sports bra in seconds leaving us both naked from the waist up. Although my forty-two-year-old body could hardly match hers. At a mere twenty-seven, her tits were still firm, buoyant and very much in the right place while mine sagged alarmingly. Still she hadn't recoiled in disgust, quite the reverse. While I returned to praising her nipples with my tongue, teeth and fingers, her hands were busy plastering mine with something delightfully cool and slippery. Bombarded by a flurry of intense sexual messages and mind-blowing sensations, my body answered each one by calling for more and more until I thought I'd combust from sheer frustration. A whole year of abstinence wasn't helping me cope with a situation way beyond my reason or anything I'd ever experienced before.

Arlene suddenly pushed me back until I had no option but to let go of her nipple. Once she had me prostrate on the cushions, and at her mercy, she covered me with her body and sealed her lips to mine.

We fitted together perfectly, breasts touching, tingling, alive with sensations, skin sliding against skin as we panted out our expressions of sexual desire. Arlene thrust her tongue into my mouth and we exchanged soft breathy moans of pleasure while we explored this new territory. When she used her knee to spread my thighs and tried to settle her weight between them I took a stand. I wasn't comfortable letting her make all the running, the butch in me liked to be in full control of the sexual journey. I rolled her over and took command of the situation.

Deciding she still wore too many clothes, I eased her tunic and leggings down her thighs my fingers gliding easily across her soft silky skin then slid both off her feet together with her sandals before I sat up, and surveyed my naked prize. Her breasts had been merely a tantalizing aperitif, the rest of her body offered the promise of a mouthwatering main course and a delicious desert. She met my gaze and her lips parted in a long dreamy sigh. Her luminescent golden eyes called me to fuck her but I held back not wanting to break the spell or finish this too soon.

I began by trailing hot kisses down her neck. Then adding various delicious adornments to the pink and green design across her chest I worked my way slowly downwards, kissing, caressing, and decorating her entire body with a feast of succulent foodstuff. While I carefully avoided the one secret place, I knew she wanted me to touch—every time I got close, she whimpered and thrashed about disturbing my artistic handiwork. For the third time in as many minutes, I held her down and re-arranged the fruit on her belly. This time she stayed still long enough for me to tuck a glistening cherry into her navel above the heart-shaped diamond stud she wore and finally add a halo of strawberries to frame her neatly trimmed mound. Arlene moaned softly when I trickled raspberry syrup over the cream on her inner thighs moving upwards, getting ever closer to her pussy. She looked an absolute picture—I felt for my cell phone, unable to resist the urge to capture this unique moment for posterity then, mission accomplished, I returned the phone to the holder attached to my belt.

All I needed now was one final magic ingredient to complete the experience in style.

I spread her thighs a little more, then with her open to my gaze, I picked up the bottle of champagne and trickled a steady stream of bubbles onto her swollen clit. Arlene's body jerked, her fingers scrunched wildly at the cushion as if she was trying to save herself from falling.

"Jaaaaaay!" Arlene's voice raised several octaves, my name flowing off her lips like musical wind chimes carried on the breeze. "I can't..." Tension rippled through Arlene's body, tightening her muscles as she fought the call of the abyss. Her movements both sensual and erotically explicit held me in their thrall. I could taste her need, her desire for release, for the moment of complete ecstasy that hovered just out of reach. I held her in suspense for as long as possible before I gave in and dribbled more champagne on her clitoris aiming at the sensitive pink tip standing proud of the hood. "Yes, oh yessssss!" Her high-pitched scream echoed around us. Then she tumbled over the edge into her climax.

She looked incredibly beautiful in the throes of release. Her eyes widened, becoming more intensely vibrant like rich tortoiseshell and her gorgeous red lips parted to allow a series of amazing sounds to escape.

My gaze dropped to focus on the pulsing center of this phenomenal reaction. I leant down and ran my tongue across her clit then lapped at the area where her juices flowed freely to mingle with the wine. She tasted divine, like honey-flavored champagne if there was such a thing. The nectar fizzed on my tongue as her orgasm built to its peak, while I held my climax off—just. Satisfying my lady always came before my own pleasure. I drove two fingers inside her slick opening then, once I got the feel of her, added a third. She kept coming, strong contractions pulled my fingers deeper. Responding to her continued expressions of pleasure, I pumped hard and fast while nursing her clit.

When I thought she'd slipped down from the high point, I slowed my hand movement settling into a gentler rhythm as I prepared to withdraw and put my mouth to good use grazing her body for tasty tidbits.

"Don't stop!" Arlene's plea came on a rasp of breath and her fingers moved in to claw at her clit. "I'm so close to...Aaah..." A violent shudder rocked her body, her muscles gripping my hand as she braced her feet on the floor and pushed up seeking deeper penetration. I hesitated, hardly believing her stamina. "Come on!" I obeyed her command with increased depth and speed Arlene echoing my movements, meeting my measured thrusts with a vigor that heralded the approach of a second powerful climax.

Arlene drifted slowly out of the orgasmic zone, her breathing relaxed, returning to its normal level before she spoke. "Oh, yes, I am totally... you are a very sexy bitch, Jay."

"So are you." I lifted my head to look into her beautiful amber eyes, returning the compliment with heartfelt appreciation.

"You ain't seen nothing yet." A wicked grin crept across Arlene's face, before she turned her attention to my remaining garments. Frantic hands attacked my jeans, tearing at the button and zipper then sliding my briefs down my thighs at the same time as the heavier denim. I kicked my boots off so she could complete the process of rendering me naked, ready, and willing, to accept whatever delights she deemed necessary to complete our night of sexual pleasures.

Arlene didn't disappoint me, her inventive use of various foods and the places she inserted them, had me crying with both the agony and the joy of total sexual gratification.

Much later, having had our excess of food fun in various rooms we finally made it into the shower. With much horseplay, we took turns lathering each other all over, paying particular attention to our erogenous zones. Arlene wound me up, teasing me into a state of heightened sexual awareness that left me wanting to take her again. I thrust Arlene against the tiled wall then lifted her up until she wrapped her legs around my waist. Our lips met in a hungry exchange of heated kisses, tongues imitating sex while our slick bodies slid sensuously together until Arlene cried out her release. God, this woman was insatiable. I had lost count of how many time she'd come—I'd had four orgasms but she was way ahead of me on that score. Not that I was complaining. I'd had a wonderful evening and, hopefully, there might be more to come before the week was through.

And so it proved.

Try as I might to return her hospitality, Arlene refused all my dinner invitations during the rest of the week, insisting I come to her house instead. "We can be ourselves here with no constraints." Arlene knew what she wanted and she got it in spades. Every evening, after my day doing the rounds of the events, I hurried through the ritual of showering and changing then made my way to her house for an evening of sexual adventures.

I left Ptown late on Sunday afternoon, well fed and totally satiated, with Arlene's parting, "maybe next year" ringing in my ears. All I could think, as I headed out to the airport for the last flight of the day, was that, next year was a very long way away.

DESIRE & DECEPTION

The throb of the agency cell phone against my thigh turned the breakfast bagel to sawdust in my mouth and sent my heartbeat racing out of control.

Fuck! Messages to this phone usually meant trouble. It'd been nine months since the last text, and I didn't want to remember what happened back then nor the loss of my long-time partner, Cal Watson in the operation that followed. My blood ran cold at the prospect of going on another assignment without Carol to watch my back. I let my glance travel idly around the diner under cover of taking a sip of coffee then set my cup down, palmed the cell and checked the message.

"You have an appointment to view 3015 Stamford Hill. If you're still interested in the property, please meet the vendor, Max Beacon, there at noon. Walker!"

The coded text translated into a meeting with another undercover agent, called Max Stamford, at three thirty in the parking lot at Beacon Hill. I expelled a steady breath, hit reply, then sent the empty message as acknowledgement and replaced the cell in the pocket of my cargo pants. This development, coming out of the blue, probably meant a new operation. Something that would require an exchange of documents or photographs, a change of cover, and possibly in view of my lone state a new partner or handler. My stomach churned nauseously, I pushed my half-eaten breakfast away and left the diner in search of fresh air.

A few minutes short of the appointed time, I slotted my aged Mustang into one of the few vacant spots in the Beacon Hill parking lot. The popular beauty spot, serving several forest trails, attracted families and serious walkers alike but I wasn't here to enjoy a lazy afternoon cookout or a hike. The milling crowds provided perfect cover for my meeting with Max Stamford and since neither the name nor the face rang any bells, I'd have to rely on him making contact.

"Kay!" I'd hardly exited the vehicle when I heard my cover name seconds before a woman launched her body into my arms and pushed me back against the hot metal hood. She smelt so good, an exotic aroma bathed my senses in spicy sandalwood overlaid with hints of cedar and lime. For a brief moment, I thought I'd died and gone to heaven. Then I recovered and cursed my slow reaction. In other circumstances, or in the wrong hands, I might easily have met a sticky end.

"Hey, Foxy Lady, you look great." She whispered my identification code as she kissed me on both cheeks then, disregarding our public location, sealed her lips to mine, cutting off my response. Jeez, this gal sure knew how to whip up a sexual tornado. Weak ass that I am I melted into the kiss, opening my mouth on her command and welcoming her inside. She tasted sweet, like a soft vanilla candy. Her tongue intertwined with mine, silky, sensuous, and so sexy. Moist heat rushed to my crotch. A compelling reminder of my long sexual hiatus. Pity we were in a public place, my throbbing cunt urged me to pursue this sudden desire to its logical conclusion. Max Stamford could fuck me any time she liked and in any way.

She eventually quit the kiss and stepped back to assess me with a lengthy sweep of keen hazel-brown eyes. Easily five ten tall her lean tanned frame carried not an ounce of fat. A dark brown T-shirt and matching plaid shorts accentuated her height. "It's so good to see you again." Max smiled, keeping up the pretense of us being longtime friends.

"You too, Max." I subdued my libido and continued her charade for the benefit of any listeners. "Yes, it's been quite a while since we last met. Are you still a keen walker?" I managed, belatedly, to include the security word from the text.

She nodded and adjusted her hat, giving me a brief flash of short, spiky, dark hair with highlights. "Shall we take a stroll now? I've got lots of news for you."

Max's idea of a stroll turned out to be more of a fast jog along a steep, densely wooded trail. My chest was on fire by the time we finally left the trees behind and halted on a rocky outcrop with a clear view across the tree canopy. I ignored the view and concentrated on coaxing air into my starved lungs.

"You're out of condition." Hardly out of breath herself, Max took a long draft from her water bottle then passed it to me. "I can see I'll have to haul your sorry ass off to the gym if we're going to be partners."

The intake of breath caught in my throat. "Partners? Since when?"

This gorgeous creature is my new partner.

I couldn't begin to get my head around complications this sexy wench might bring to my life both professional and private.

"Today. I've just come from a meet with Laxton. He said we'd be perfect together."

I smiled. "Did he?" Laxton was a wily old fox. I'd known my *Uncle Tom* all my life, since he and dad had worked together during my childhood. I hadn't known then they were undercover agents, not until dad died and Tom Laxton came to see me—and recruited me in dad's place.

"Yes he did. He reckons you're very good at everything you do. I can't wait to test his theory."

I blew an imaginary kiss to Tom for his faith in me. "It's nice to be appreciated."

"Anyway, Laxton also gave me details of our new assignment. We're going after Charlie Brown's wife. Apparently, the delectable Poppy has a penchant for her own sex, though she's still in the closet, of course, and relatively inexperienced." Max grinned broadly, her even white teeth flashing like a toothpaste ad in the sunlight. "I'm sure between us we can change that. According to the latest reports from the people on the ground, the thing our Poppy enjoys most is a threesome with an experienced couple. If we can get her into bed and coming hard there's no telling what she may let slip about hubby's little enterprise."

"So you and I are going to..." Words failed me. The thought of working up close and very personal with this gorgeous sexy butch sent erotic shivers cascading down my spine. However unprofessional my thoughts I couldn't wait to get her into my bed.

"You got it in one. Laxton reckons we'll make a perfect couple and he's even offered to pay for a week's vacation to give us time to get properly acquainted before we move into our new home and take up a corporate membership at the exclusive club our Poppy frequents." She led me around a large rock to a secluded ledge that offered a natural seat.

I sat, grateful to take the weight off my trembling limbs. "A paid vacation?" *Laxton must be getting soft in his old age.* I leant back against the warm rock.

"Yeah! I know..." Max shrugged and dropped onto the ledge beside me our thighs touching. "He originally said we could choose anywhere we liked but quickly retracted his offer when I suggested the Virgin Islands, so I settled for a quiet condo he owns at Virginia Beach instead."

"Sounds good to me." I turned my head to look at Max. She had the most attractive eyes I'd ever seen—I wanted to drown in those captivating, flecked, pools of desire. Hell, I wanted to do more than that, it wasn't just her eyes that dissolved my insides into a gooey mess and turned my legs to jelly.

"Me too. It'll be like a honeymoon." A mischievous smile played across her lips and lit up her eyes with twinkling stars. "We can walk, talk, swim and get to know one another intimately."

"How intimately?" My equilibrium shaken, I held her hypnotic gaze. "If we're going to pose as a couple, strong enough to convince and attract Poppy, then we'll need to be rock solid and comfortable in our sexual relationship." I wanted to establish the nature of our partnership from the outset. Since I doubted if I'd survive very long with irresistible temptation for company if we had to confine our sexual encounters to work.

"I know. We have to be totally in tune with each other's needs. Like this..." Max reached for me, her kiss gentle yet firm.

Then her lips drifted from my mouth down my neck into my cleavage. I surrendered to the exquisite delight of her soft kisses on my heated skin. Her hat fell off and I tangled my fingers in her hair, holding her close. We fell sideways with Max on top of me and her weight nestled comfortably between my thighs.

The buttons on my shirt came undone with barely a pause then she freed one tit from the confines of my sports bra and closed her mouth over the hardened nipple.

Oh! Such sweet ecstasy. "Yes!" I moaned aloud and thrust my tit hard into her face. I wanted her to exert her butch authority, to take me, to fuck me right here, right now.

She lifted her head from my chest and gave me a long meaningful look. "Yes, what? Tell me what you want."

"You!" Breathless, hot, wet, my heart pumping, I could hardly force the words from my parched lips. "Fuck me now. Please! I'm burning up inside. Make me come like I've never come before."

Max smiled. "I thought you'd never ask." Deft hands maneuvered me into position and removed my cargo shorts. She spread my thighs and took her time exploring my crotch. Sure fingers probed and circled wet cotton until I wanted to scream with frustration. Then she ripped the fabric apart and her fingers found my clit. My silent scream became one of unbridled pleasure. I spread my thighs wider and thrust my ass forward to meet her caress full on.

"That's it, baby. Let it all out," Max cooed, thrusting deep into my throbbing slit then curling her fingers, palm upwards, as she withdrew. An incredible sensation gripped me. The sheer magic of her touch, her actions, drove me wild.

A faint trembling began at my extremities then crept slowly inwards gathering in intensity as it neared my core. Max upped her pace and my body responded. Unable to control my movements I thrashed about, my fingers scrabbling wildly at my clit until Max pushed my hand aside and took control there with her mouth. She teased, sucked, and licked, curling her warm tongue around my throbbing clit like it was a precious jewel or the most succulent delight in the whole wide world.

"Oh, fuck...I'm..." My orgasm erupted from deep inside, just like the fiery volcano's I'd seen on TV. Still Max didn't let up she kept pumping me, her deep, satisfying thrusts projecting my climax into the stratosphere. The unparalleled intensity and duration took me to new heights and left my body boneless, free of tension, and totally drained.

Finally, Max sat back on her heels a wide smile on her face. "I think that proves our sexual compatibility."

I nodded. Too emotional to speak. Tears clouded my vision, I'd searched all my life for the perfect butch lover and now Tom had unwittingly picked her for me. I must remember to send him a bottle of his favorite Bourbon as a thank you. Despite our short acquaintance, I knew it in my heart Max was the one, and prayed to God that we'd have time together, time to explore and enjoy our relationship, before fate or the agency split us up.

"Shall we go?" Max glanced at her watch. "It's at the very least a five hour drive from here to Virginia Beach and after that little appetizer I can't wait much longer to take you to bed. As it is, I'm thinking we may need to stop en route for a quick nibble to keep us going.

We returned to town separately, where I grabbed a few clothes and some other personal stuff from my apartment then transferred everything to Max's truck, before garaging my car for the duration.

* * * *

Five weeks later, with our quasi honeymoon a wonderful, though distant memory, we'd settled into our new life, and established the cover provided by Laxton. Max's role, as a software engineer, meant she supposedly worked from home while I played the fun-loving wife for all it was worth. In fact, Max did spend a lot of time on the computer mainly logging the useful information we gleaned from our surveillance into a central database and keeping track of the wider operation. Our regular visits to the club, both singly and together, attracted no adverse attention from either clientele or staff. Now it was just a matter of waiting for Poppy to show an interest in sharing our bed.

We soon established that she spent most days there either chatting with friends or using the extensive facilities. A chauffeur-driven car delivered her to the club each morning and collected her most nights—she never drove herself although she did stay overnight on occasions. Poppy didn't work out, unlike most members, instead, she preferred all the girlie stuff, like using the tanning beds, having her body plastered in gloop, getting a full-body massage or just having her hair, face and nails done. With the aim of getting closer to her, I gritted my teeth and booked into several hair and beauty sessions timing my appointments to coincide with hers.

"Hi there! I'm Poppy." She broke the ice as we sat side by side in the hair salon one morning.

"Hello, Poppy." I offered a friendly smile but no more, we wanted her to make the running and in particular for her to initiate any sexual activity.

"I've seen you around the club with..." She carefully avoided committing herself to an opinion on our status.

"Max, my partner, and I'm Kay." I waved my left hand bearing an engraved silver commitment ring. Max had bought matching rings while we were at Virginia Beach, insisting we both wear one to give truth to our lie. "We've been together seven years, it's our anniversary next week." I was pleased to hear that my voice carried total conviction.

"Cool." Poppy nodded, smiling. She idly flicked the baby-blonde curls away from her eyes then let her gaze drift to dwell on my cleavage. She circled her lips with the tip of her tongue, the sexy gesture a clear indication of her interest in me. "You look real good together."

"Thank you." We were good in every way. A shockwave suddenly ripped through my body when I realized with how far from mere work partners we'd become over these last few weeks. Sex played an enormous part in our life—we couldn't get enough of each other in or out of bed. Laxton would have had fifty fits had he witnessed us having a quickie in the kitchen during breakfast just this morning. Despite having had our regular morning sexual workout in the shower, we were hungry for each other again not half an hour later.

Poppy's smile widened. "Will you have lunch with me when we finish up here?"

"Yes, I'd love to." My heart performed a little jig—we were in at last. I couldn't wait to call Max with the good news. Hopefully our sojourn here would soon be finished.

* * * *

"From a quiet corner table in the bar, Max and I watched Poppy get more than a little tipsy on a succession of sickly-looking pink cocktails. With her neat little ass perched precariously on a high bar stool she appeared oblivious to our presence although I suspected she was using the mirrored bar display to check us out.

Earlier, over our lobster salad and champagne lunch, Poppy had made a concerted effort to woo me. She'd found as many excuses as possible to touch me on the knee or the arm, accidentally catching my tit whenever she could, and fluttered her long eyelashes suggestively. When she finally came out and told me she enjoyed sex with women, I responded in a firm yet friendly manner. "I'm really flattered, Poppy, but I don't cheat on Max." Poppy shrugged and fell silent. I cursed our decision to play it this way thinking I'd blown the whole operation, then she remarked, "You don't need to cheat, Max is welcome to join in the action. Three is much more fun anyway." I grinned and nodded. "True, we're not averse to a little threesomes action either." Poppy's delight at my agreement was too pathetically childish for words. I quickly excused myself and returned home to consult with Max on the plan of campaign.

Suddenly Poppy launched herself off the bar stool and headed on unsteady limbs in our direction. "Showtime!" Max grabbed my hand, squeezed it tight, and then whispered, "Whatever happens tonight, don't forget I love you," into my ear. My heart jolted in my chest. Something in her tone told me Max wasn't kidding, this declaration was a scary development for us, both as a couple and for our working partnership, but Poppy arrived at our table before I could respond.

"Hey, you two." Her words ran together. "I feel like some action. Wanna fuck?"

Jeez! I fought down a gasp of surprise. Poppy was some crazy bitch in heat.

"Maybe." Max, being the perfect butch, stood and pulled out a chair for her. "We were actually just about to leave."

"Don't go, please." Poppy rocked in her seat, her stacked tits swayed from side to side mimicking her movement. "I'm feeling real sexy tonight and I wanna get laid."

"What about your husband?" Max offered up token resistance. "Won't he be waiting for you?"

"Nah!" Poppy shook her head. "He's away on business this week, making lots of lovely money. Besides, he doesn't do it right…and I wanna come so bad."

I fought to keep a straight face made even more difficult when a muffled snort from Max followed Poppy's admission of her unsatisfactory sex life. Poor Poppy.

"In that case allow us to do the honors." Max stood. "Will you come home with us or do you have somewhere else we can go?" We'd already discussed this at length and planned to get her into our spare room where both a camera and sound recording were already set up but didn't want to appear too obvious. We'd only have this one opportunity to get her talking. Once she sobered up she'd likely realize her mistake or somebody would realize it for her, and our chance of screwing her for information would be gone forever.

"I have a suite here but..." Poppy glanced furtively around the near empty bar and shook her head. "Nah! They spy on me. I...I wanna go with you."

As previously arranged, Max brought our car to a blind spot near the side entrance while I steered Poppy from the bar with as little fuss as possible. Then we took a detour via the restroom and the terrace to avoid the security cameras. The trip home took scant minutes. Once there Max drove straight into the garage and closed the automatic door before we got Poppy out of the car.

"This is nice." Poppy flopped onto our spare bed and wriggled around until she kicked off her heels.

Her miniskirt rode up in the process to reveal both the lack of underwear and a neatly waxed pussy. "Come here, sexy." She reached for Max, pulled her down onto the bed and started tearing at her clothes.

I took the opportunity to start the recorders then undressed to my bra and briefs.

"Slow down, Poppy." Max held her hands, firmly halting the frantic tearing at clothes while she still retained her underwear. "Just keep still and let us give you a good time."

"Fuck me. I wanna come."

"We will. You will, I promise." Max undid Poppy's shirt, pulled it clear of her arms and then traced the outline of her artificially enhanced breasts where they spilled from the miniscule cups of a lacy bra.

I slid onto the bed on Poppy's other side and slipped the catch on her bra.

"So how do you like your sex Poppy?" Max adopted a sultry tone. "We've got handcuffs, a nice silk flogger. Or maybe you prefer us to fuck you with a strap-on or a dildo? You can have whatever you want. Your wish is our command."

"Handcuffs." Poppy sounded awed. "You gonna tie me up?"

"Only if you ask us nicely." I waved a pair of fur-covered cuffs in front of her then stroked them up the soft flesh of her inner thigh. "You can get out whenever you want."

"Yes please." She held out her wrists. I clipped the shackles to them then attached the other end to the brass bed rail. Poppy giggled and wriggled her body, clearly excited by the novelty of playing sexual games. "You gonna flog me now?"

"All in good time." Max wet her fingers and manipulated one of Poppy's nipples. "Where did you say your husband went on business?"

"Mmmm…Not sure. Maybe Colombia…that's where all the action is."

I whisked the soft silk flogger lightly across her other breast. Poppy sighed, her nipples hardening visibly. "Really? How did he travel there?" Silken threads flicked Poppy's stomach.

Her body jerked. "He…he went to Florida for the fishing."

My hand drifted lower to draw the soft strands lightly across her mound. "Oh, yes!" She groaned.

I smiled. "You said he went to Colombia."

"Did I?" She opened her thighs wide inviting me to touch her clit. "No…I don't know…I just remember hearing him say something about a private jet and Colombia."

Interesting. I met Max's gaze. *An odd route for somebody to take from here to South America.* I rewarded

Poppy for the information by running the flogger once across her clit. She bucked wildly.

"When is he due home?"

Poppy shook he head. "Next week, maybe... I never know when...until he gets back. His cell phone won't work from the boat."

Or, more likely, he didn't want to risk a traced signal leading to awkward questions.

I teased her inner thigh with the flogger. "Does your husband go away on these trips regularly?" She was really wet, ready, and so willing. Her pussy pulsed invitingly. It wouldn't take much to make her come but that wasn't the object of this exercise at least not until we'd milked her of every last scrap of information.

"Not often enough..." Poppy sighed and tried to rub her clit against my wrist. "I'm thirsty...need a drink?"

In my opinion, she'd already had more than enough. However to keep her happy I gave her a glass of the cranberry juice heavily laced with vodka I'd prepared earlier and put ready on the nightstand. She downed the generous measure in a single thirsty gulp.

"How often?" I removed the empty glass from Poppy's lips and glanced at Max who nodded and grinned. We were doing well but time was running out. The likelihood was she'd either pass out or clam up within the hour.

"Four…maybe five times a year."

Max moved to caress Poppy's other thigh. "Who does he meet on these trips?"

"Oh! Yes!" Poppy spread her legs wider, inviting us to fuck her. "Somebody called Alberto, he runs that end of the operation for Marco."

We ignored her invitation and continued to stroke her thighs while keeping well clear of her clit.

"And the money side, is that Alberto too?"

"No…I don't know…I think Marco looks after the money." She giggled and put her mouth close to Max's ear. "This is so funny…do you know what he does? He washes the dirty money to make it clean."

"Really!" A grin played at the corner of Max's mouth. "Where does he do that?"

"At the club, silly." Poppy chuckled. "In the washing machine with the towels."

I raised my brow and Max confirmed with a shrug that the club wasn't on our radar. This was good stuff. Poppy certainly lived up to her dizzy blonde image. From her answers, it appeared she got most of her information second hand or from listening in to one-sided phone conversations. Marco probably kept her in the dark for a good reason. His drug and money laundering operation depended on secrecy.

As a reward, I reached for the ten-inch dong, flicked on the power. Max held her thighs apart while I rubbed the throbbing pink latex against the soft flesh. Poppy's body bucked and she started to whimper. "Fuck me, please...I'm so..."

"Soon." Max smoothed her brow with a cool damp pad. "You need to tell us who Marco works for first. Give us a name."

"No names...sssecret...gotta keep his name sssh..." Poppy placed a finger to her lips. "Jago is a big man...very dangerous."

A cold shiver snaked down my spine. "Jago who?" I gave her thigh another blast with the pulsating dildo. "Does Jago have another name?"

"Marco said..." Poppy frowned and shook her head. "He said Jago lived up to his name. Moral...Moral less...he was joking, right."

"Probably." A dark shadow played across Max's face. We'd both heard the name Jago Morales. Who hadn't in our business? The big time drug baron who'd disappeared in mysterious circumstances some ten years previously, presumed murdered. Now, suddenly, he was back on the scene or more likely, somebody else had cleverly assumed his identity. I'd only ever seen a hazy black and white photo of Morales taken in the late seventies.

My common sense told me it couldn't possibly be the same man, the man who'd killed my dad, he'd be in his dotage now but I needed to know, to be sure. "Poppy." I shook her arm. "Have you seen this Jago?"

"Steady, Kay. Poppy isn't our enemy. We're here to have fun, remember."

I shrugged Max's hand off my shoulder. "You don't have to tell me that but I need to know if ..."

"Yes, I understand." Max leaned across and dropped a light kiss on my lips to silence my protest then she whispered. "Let's make Poppy feel good first—we can talk later."

Poppy wriggled her body against me and my hand made contact with her breast. "Fuck! I wanna have a good time…"

Shit! I'd almost blown my cover.

Thanks to Max's quick thinking, however, I was off the hook. I wanted to hug her for stopping me from making a complete mess of things but she was busy elsewhere.

"You got it babe." Max had taken over the dildo I'd dropped and now she knelt between Poppy's thighs her voice softly seductive like a porn star teasing the viewer to a climax. "I'm going to fuck you real good. You're going to come so long, and so hard, you won't know where you are. But first, you have to answer one little question. Where does Jago Morales live?" She touched the throbbing dong to Poppy's clit.

"Eeeeow!" Her hips shot off the bed. "Please! Fuck me…" She begged and then her body sank back down to the mattress, writhing sinuously.

Max grinned. "Sure, baby…I can't wait to bury my fat dick in your slick pussy. Just tell me where to find Jago Morales and I'll take you to paradise."

"I don't know." The breath rasped in Poppy's throat. "I think he moves… Marco talks of many places…an island off the Cuban coast, Panama City, Santa something and…I forget."

This information was probably the best we could hope for given Poppy's drunken state and better than we had already. Max met my gaze and I nodded my agreement to finish her off.

I pushed Poppy's thighs up and apart resting her ankles on Max's shoulders then Max drove the dildo deep into her slit.

"Yes!" Poppy shouted out her pleasure.

Slow and deep, fast and hard, Max worked relentlessly sliding the dong in and out. Poppy moaned and thrashed about, getting closer to her orgasm yet resisting the fall. Finally, I stepped in to end her distress by massaging her swollen clit.

Within seconds, she let go a piercing scream and fell over the edge. Max pushed the dildo in real deep one last time then we sat back and let nature take its course. Poppy's body bucked and trembled for ages, tears flowed from her eyes as she sobbed out her relief. Poor woman. I actually felt quite sorry for her. I reached out, unlocked the cuffs and released her arms then left Poppy to come down from her high while I got dressed. Max followed my example. We needed to move fast, to get Poppy back to the club and our personal stuff packed up then disappear before the shit hit the proverbial fan. A clean-up squad would move in to deal with everything else.

Nearly forty-eight hours later we let ourselves into Laxton's secluded Virginia Beach condo grateful to be free of work and the ever-present dangers our job entailed, and ready to relax after our long drive. We'd stopped many times for comfort breaks, once to hand over the valuable information to another operative, swap vehicles and lose our old identities and one other time when hunger got the better of us.

"Come here." Max kicked the door shut with the heel of her boot, grabbed me by the arms and trapped me against the wall with her hard body. She sealed her mouth to mine, her tongue snaking between my lips, making our bond complete. My body tuned immediately to the drumbeat of her pulse, leaving me hot, wet, and very ready to both give and receive, just as it had last night. Max had discovered a secluded grassy plateau high in the mountains where we spent a couple of wonderful hours satisfying our hunger and relieving the tension of the operation. There I'd become addicted to fucking outdoors under a clear starry sky, it added a new dimension to our sexual pleasure.

Max's hands dropped to cup my ass, pulling me close and lifting up me until I wrapped my legs around her hips. I tangled my fingers in her hair straining for even closer contact and she moaned softly into my mouth. Max pushed harder grinding her body deep into my crotch until I could hardly think straight. I wanted satisfaction. To feel her hand deep inside my slit guiding me with her magic touch to that special orgasm, the one that left me boneless and drained.

I tore my mouth from hers. "Fuck me!" I gasped, panting, breathless. "Do it now! I can't wait!"

"With pleasure, Foxy Lady." Max chuckled then scooped me up and carried me through to the bathroom. Her deft hands quickly dispensed with our clothes before she led me under the warm refreshing spray in the double shower stall.

We soaped each other lavishly, the ritual massaging of skin with silky soft lather always added to our pleasure and increased our insatiable desire. Then Max slammed me against the tiled wall, and our slick bodies melded breast to breast in familiar harmony. She trailed hungry kisses down my throat then back up to capture my mouth while my cunt throbbed out its own urgent message. I wanted her so badly pain tore at every nerve ending.

She used one knee to shove my legs apart and then drilled her fingers deep inside my aching slit almost lifting me off the tiled floor. "Oh, Kay I'm…" Max shuddered into silence, grabbed a handful of my hair and yanked my head back then traced a path down my throat with her hot lips and used her teeth to graze one of my nipples.

My cunt convulsed tightly around her fingers. "Fuck! Yes!" She pumped harder, faster, deeper, her need for completion transferring to me and I worked my body in time with her thrusts. Max reached up to kiss me, forcing my lips apart she plunged her tongue into my mouth. I couldn't control my body, the shaking, my legs buckled and I collapsed in a heap on the shower floor taking Max down with me. After a few moments, she reached up and cut the spray then held me tight until all vestiges of trembling ceased.

Then Max wrapped me in a large towel and carried me through to the bedroom where we clung to each other for a long time in total silence just sharing intimate kisses. Irrationally, I wanted to stop the clock, to make this night to go on forever so we'd never again have to face the uncertainty of working undercover or in a hostile environment.

We needed to make the most of our brief spell of freedom. Danger was only a phone call away. Sooner or later, the cell phone would ring again, testing our love and lives to the limit.

LOVING ELLIE

" . . . and this is your room."

Taylor Hendry emerged from her trance to focus on Ellie Lawrence, who stood just inside the room with her back against the white paneled door.

Ellie's sensuous beauty took her breath away, and that cerise miniskirt with a coordinated rainbow chiffon top did wonders for her figure. Taylor inhaled the hint of intoxicating perfume that drifted on the current of warm air and barely managed to resist the urge to move closer. She longed to taste those inviting candy-pink lips, to wrap that gorgeous body in her arms and hold it close, before she ripped those sexy garments off with her teeth and...

No! However horny she was, she mustn't go there. Taylor tore her gaze away from Ellie and attempted to control her labored breathing. She took her time examining the spacious room that would be her base for the next six months.

Late evening sunlight filtered through billowing voile curtains to bathe everything in soft amber light, complementing the predominately ivory and gold décor. An antique brass bedstead, framed by built-in wardrobe units, dominated the far end of the room while closer to the door a large couch, an entertainment unit and ample office space completed the picture.

With a smile on her lips, she turned back to meet Ellie's expectant gaze. "What a lovely room...in fact the whole apartment is perfect. I'm sure I'll be very comfortable here." In truth, she'd hardly taken in any of the grand tour because she'd had her gaze fixed firmly on the sexy sway of Ellie's ass as she preceded her around the apartment.

Ellie returned her smile and stepped in to give her a hug. "It's really great to have you here. Sam already told me so much about you, I feel like I've know you forever."

Taylor blanched and pulled out of the embrace. Damn! Given that Samantha Crighton knew far too much about her past for comfort, that loose mouth of hers could do a whole lot of damage to a girl's reputation. She'd left the world of promiscuity and hardcore BDSM behind after their college days unlike Sam.

Just how much detail had Sam revealed?

She studied Ellie's sweet face searching for clues, but those sparkling hazel eyes framed by delicious long, dark, lashes gave nothing away.

"Sam told me plenty about you too." Taylor's gaze lingered upon Ellie's luscious curves before sweeping back up to her face. "But I reckon she omitted as much as she told."

Ellie broke eye contact and dipped her head, but not in time to hide the virginal blush that swept up her neck and over her cheeks. After a moment, she looked back up and gave a tentative smile. "I'll leave you to unpack while I get supper and then, if you're up for it, we'll hit the town and I'll show you a few of my favorite nightspots."

"Thanks, I'd like that."

"Great!" Ellie turned away and sashayed elegantly down the hallway the spiked heels and mini skirt giving her long shapely legs star billing. Taylor's heart changed gear, missing several beats along the way. She waited until Ellie turned the corner before reaching down to pick up her bag and carry it over the threshold.

Without Ellie around to distract her, Taylor took the time to explore her surroundings. Sam, the colleague, with whom she'd swapped places on an exchange posting, had promised her that she'd love everything about her temporary home, and she hadn't exaggerated. Who wouldn't fall in love with this luxurious riverside apartment, or Ellie Lawrence for that matter? Not to mention the extra bonus of no lengthy commute, since the apartment was within easy walking distance of the Marchant's Bank head office on Canary Wharf.

She hummed a little tune whilst unpacking the bare essentials, including the pink tote bag that contained her favorite toys. Taylor had a feeling they might come in very handy during her stay in London. The only drawback to this seemingly perfect arrangement was Ellie, Sam's old school friend and long time housemate.

Now that she'd finally met Ellie, Taylor understood why Sam felt so protective of her. She sighed, recalling Sam's explicit warning not to mess with Ellie's emotions unless her intentions were serious. Unfortunately, Sam knew her too well, from their wild college days. She knew her penchant for tall, dark, sexy, femmes and she had to admit Ellie fitted that bill to a tee. With her cropped dark hair, sparkling hazel eyes and a gorgeous body that promised a feast of enjoyment, she was very easy on the eye. Then there was the way Ellie kept looking at her, from the moment she'd walked in the door—sort of goofy, yet hungry, as if she wanted to eat her, it was enough to send a girl wild with frustration.

Sweet innocent Ellie was far too attractive for her own good. Taylor glanced down at the bag of toys in her hand. She had no doubt Ellie would run a mile if confronted with the contents. A brief smile flitted across her lips as she pictured Ellie spread-eagle on the ivory silk quilt, her wrists and ankles bound to the brass rails of the bed whilst she drove her into a frenzy of desire with her little collection of handcuffs, plugs and floggers. Not that there was much chance of that happening. Taylor clamped her thighs together to trap the heady rush of moist heat flooding into her pussy. She quickly tucked the bag into the top drawer of the nightstand. *Out of sight, out of mind.* A long breath escaped through her teeth then she turned toward the en-suite bathroom carrying her bag of waterproof shower toys.

She must play a waiting game and see how everything worked out before getting her panties in a knot. Maybe time would solve this dilemma. No, Taylor shook her head. Relying on time to provide the right outcome didn't always solve a difficult problem, as she knew from experience. She'd lost out before by leaving things to chance. Taylor snapped her eyes shut to dismiss the image that had haunted her dreams for nearly a year.

Seeing Julia in the arms of another woman, especially a hard-faced bitch like Ray had been bad enough. Then learning that she'd lost Julia by being too cautious had driven a stake deep into her heart. Ellie Lawrence, however, posed a very different problem. Taylor sighed. If she rushed headlong into temptation before Ellie was ready for the taking, she'd be courting certain disaster. On the other hand, though, could she really manage to keep her hands to herself indefinitely?

Taylor considered that question again as she stepped out from under the shower to massage sandalwood body wash into her wet skin.

Just thinking about Ellie in this context was an enormous mistake. She cut the spray, and let her horny mind run with the fantasy of Ellie's hands on her body.

Fingers circled her breasts, now slick with the creamy fragrant soap, molded the soft flesh and teased the nipples into hard buds. Taylor groaned wanting more, much more. With her back against the shower screen, she slid down until she was sitting comfortably, her legs spread wide. Her body trembled in anticipation of the pleasure to come from her seeking fingers as they traced a path through the silky bubbles from her breasts down toward her aching clit. Taylor's breath caught and she bit her lip when they stopped short of full contact, just teasing the fine curls and building up the excitement.

When the wait became unbearable, she rose to her knees and with a forward thrust of her hips impaled herself on the waterproof vibrator, already attached to the shower tray with suckers. An uninhibited cry of pleasure echoed off the tiled walls as she took the full length deep inside with one hard thrust, her pussy welcoming the familiar velvet-soft shaft with a firm grasp.

She paused, to allow the vibrator work its magic before, imagining it was Ellie's fist, she rode out the climax like a woman possessed.

Her release came in a violent explosion of lights and nerve tingling contractions and it was several minutes before she could summon up enough energy to complete her shower and dry her hair then slip into the black pants and printed shirt she'd chosen to wear for this first night out on the town with Ellie.

* * * *

They soon settled into a comfortable routine. Taking it in turns to cook supper and deal with the boring but essential chores before going out to a club or a function. When she discovered that Ellie's job, as a journalist on a leading glossy magazine, netted her regular invitations to dressy events Taylor was thankful that she'd had the foresight to pack her only designer outfit. The go anywhere black silk evening pants suit teamed easily with a variety of shirts and simple vests to cover any occasion. After just a couple of weeks, she knew she'd miss the high life when she returned to rural Scotland. She got a real buzz rubbing shoulders with the rich and famous, those celebrities she'd only ever seen on TV or gracing the cover of a magazine.

She'd also miss spending her leisure time with Ellie. They got on so well, they might easily have been friends for their entire lives rather than two short weeks. Although being around Ellie required stamina. Keeping up with her limitless energy and unbounded enthusiasm for life, not to mention the enduring the sexual tension she stirred up, was exhausting.

So far, Taylor had resisted the urge to hit on her, aided by regular forays into her toy bag. The toys, however, were now beginning to lose their efficacy.

So much so, that Taylor had even considered making a late night visit to the lesbian bar, she'd discovered in nearby Limehouse. However, when she considered the proposal seriously, Taylor realized that a one-night stand wouldn't begin to satisfy the hunger gnawing at her gut. She wanted Ellie or nobody.

Especially when Ellie looked so sexy and desirable in that slinky midnight blue two-piece she was wearing for tonight's charity function.

Taylor had barely taken her eyes off Ellie the whole night. Her damp thong bore witness to the throbbing mess her body had become just watching Ellie flirting with a succession of high profile celebrities. Right now after much hugging and kissing, she was deep in conversation with Ariadne Kouris, the Greek born film star.

Why doesn't Ellie look at me like that?

As if sensing her mood, Ellie suddenly glanced around the ballroom and beckoned Taylor to her side.

"Have you met Ariadne Kouris?"

When Taylor admitted she hadn't had that pleasure, Ellie performed the introduction then kissed the woman full on the lips before Ariadne moved away.

"We should grab a table and order our drinks before the auction starts." Ellie linked arms with Taylor and drew her toward the front of stage, where a number of round tables were already set up complete with pale gold table linen and crystal champagne flutes.

Ellie made a beeline for one of the large tables, and soon had all twelve places filled with friends. Taylor buried her disappointment that they weren't alone and joined in the lively banter while the MC got proceedings under way.

When the first lot, a hunky actor from a popular drama series, arrived on stage, his modesty covered by a nothing more than a leather thong, the high-pitched catcalls from the predominantly female audience drowned out her gasp of surprise. Having never attended a slave auction before Taylor had great difficulty following the hectic bidding. Next up was an eighties pop star who went for peanuts compared to his predecessor.

Several more lots came and were sold for varying amounts then a murmur, like a swarm of bees on a summers afternoon, buzzed through the audience.

Ariadne Kouris strutted onto the stage on six-inch heels, to thunderous applause. She'd shed her fabulous gold evening gown in favor of a risqué black and pink teddy and fishnet stockings.

The bidding was brisk, soon reaching a four-figure sum. A smartly dressed forty-something woman from the adjoining table eventually outbid her rivals and rushed up on stage to claim her prize accompanied by loud cheers. Ariadne paused to kiss several people as she and the woman returned to the table. When she reached Ellie, Ariadne leant close and whispered something in her ear that made Ellie smile then they exchanged a meaningful kiss.

Were Ellie and Ariadne in a relationship? Taylor frowned. Jealousy gnawed at her restraint and settled like a lead weight near her midriff. How could she begin to compete with someone as rich and beautiful as Ariadne Kouris?

For two long weeks she'd held back from making a move on Ellie and she didn't know how much more torture she could take.

* * * *

"Oops!" Ellie giggled as she ricocheted off the doorframe straight into Taylor's arms, a tingle of excitement shot through her body and ignited a fire in her pussy as one flailing hand made contact with Taylor's soft breast. "We really shouldn't have finished that second bottle of champagne."

"We?" Taylor raised a questioning eyebrow. "You drank most of it by yourself. I hardly touched a drop."

Ellie frowned. "Did I...?" She tried to focus her mind. A whole bottle sounded scary, and way above her normal limit of two or at the very most, three small glasses of wine. Although the ruinously expensive Bollinger champagne they'd drunk at tonight's charity do hadn't seemed nearly as potent as her usual tipple. Besides which, she had definitely needed something to fight off the strange desire to jump another woman.

Was the drink clouding her judgment?

No—she was sober enough to know her own mind. An icy shiver trickled down her spine as the realization dawned. For the first time in her life, she wanted to have full-on mad passionate sex with a woman. Not just any woman either, she wanted to fuck Taylor Hendry so bad it hurt.

Something incredible happened to her the moment this stunning woman walked into her life. Her heartbeat raced into overdrive again just reliving the split second when she'd connected with Taylor's iridescent cobalt-blue eyes. Then, when her gaze had swept over that sexy body clad in a gray pin-stripe business suit a switch had flipped in her brain.

"Yes, you did." Taylor steered her firmly across the room towards the sofa. "Here, sit down and I'll make us some coffee."

Already unsteady on her feet, Ellie caught her heel in the carpet and fell backwards onto the floor taking Taylor down on top of her.

Their eyes met and locked and the world stopped turning.

All the air whooshed out of her lungs leaving Ellie a prisoner trapped in a web of incredible mind-blowing sensation, unable to move or breathe, drowning in a maelstrom of erotic imagery.

Then their lips touched and the electric shock brought her world back into sharp reality.

"Oh…" Ellie expelled her mortification on a ragged breath.

Could I really have kissed another woman?

No. For a start, that fleeting touch of lips wasn't a proper kiss, and she didn't even know which of them had initiated it but it had happened and they couldn't take it back.

"I'm so sorry… I…"

"Shush." Taylor silenced her apology by resting one slender finger against her lips. After a moment it moved, circling her lips slowly until they parted under the gentle pressure. Something prompted Ellie's tongue to snake out and touch the tip and then, emboldened, she drew the whole finger into her mouth. Sucking, savoring, sweeping its length with her tongue until overwhelmed by desire, she bit down on it.

Taylor's groan rang in her ears, as if from a long way away—the sound echoing her own rising excitement.

How did one become so aroused from such a simple act?

Her clit throbbed. No, not just her clit, Ellie marveled how swiftly and urgently her whole body had responded to the stimuli.

She shifted position, spreading her legs slightly and raising her hips to allow Taylor's weight to nestle more comfortably between her thighs. Although even this wasn't enough to assuage the pain of intense frustration, there was still a barrier between them.

She yearned to rip away every scrap of clothing, to experience the feeling of skin on skin, to feast upon Taylor's warm honey scented body until it exploded against her tongue.

Jeez! Where had that come from?

Ellie shook her head, confused by the unexpected strength of her feelings, and the even stranger places her mind was wandering. Taking a firm grip, she reined in her libido. She was living in fantasy land even contemplating a sexual relationship with Taylor—especially as she wasn't entirely convinced that Taylor was in fact a lesbian. Sure, she nearly always wore pants suits and shirts, but she wasn't overtly butch, like Sam, just not very feminine. She was tempted to ask but this wasn't the sort of topic one could raise, without the possibility of causing offence.

How did one tell?

She gnawed at her bottom lip. Apart from the obvious dykes, who openly proclaimed their sexuality to the world, most of the lesbians she knew were fairly discrete and certainly didn't walk around with 'I am a lesbian' tattooed across their forehead for all to see.

What is happening to me?

Ellie tried to establish some rational explanation for her wantonness. Sure, frustration might play a part. She'd deliberately kept a low profile since her engagement ended in a scandal, a month before the wedding, and her ex, Paul Antrobus, publicly cited her frigidity as just cause for his shameless behavior with his secretary. Ellie shuddered, recalling the awful moment when she'd read those lies and bitter recriminations splashed all over the pages of what until that point had been her favorite gossip magazine.

However, two years of self-imposed celibacy failed to explain why her sexual preference had shifted from men to women or to be strictly accurate, one woman in particular. She'd never felt this way about any other woman, not even Sam.

I am not a lesbian.

Ellie chanted the mantra repeatedly in her head, but somehow the words had a hollow ring to them. She had to face the sobering fact that this obsession with Taylor was like an out of control juggernaut, careering through her well ordered life, destroying everything she understood and trusted about herself in the process. And she hadn't the faintest idea where it was headed or how to apply the brakes.

Insidious voices played inside Ellie's head, urging her on.

Maybe I don't have to.

Surely, I can indulge myself, just for a few minutes, or maybe a few hours.

Go on a voyage of discovery and see where it takes me.

Shyly she reached out to touch Taylor's face. Her fingers drifted across high cheekbones down her neck then on through the valley between her breasts teasing open each tiny iridescent pearl button on her evening shirt as she went. All the time her gaze never strayed from Taylor's, watching, waiting, for some sign of rejection.

Ellie moistened suddenly dry lips with the tip of her tongue. This was virgin territory, so to speak, with no roadmap to guide her way she had only a vague idea how to reach the ultimate destination. Taylor clearly didn't intend to help her but neither had she done anything to hinder so, although terrified of putting a foot wrong and messing things up, she'd have to trust in her instinct.

The breath caught in her throat when the front fastening on Taylor's bra gave way and both breasts spilled out into her hands. A soft fragrance, sultry yet sort of mysterious drifted off her skin, reminding Ellie of the exotic blooms in her grandmother's conservatory.

Holy cow! I've really stepped over the line now.

Without thinking of the consequences, her thumbs moved to caress Taylor's nipples. As she manipulated them into hard buds, Ellie longed to take one of the jeweled tips into her mouth, to feel them grow, and experience the sweetness on her tongue but shyness prevented her putting that desire into practice.

An all-consuming fire infused Ellie's body. Her breasts felt heavy, the nipples both tingling and aching, while her pussy throbbed out its own message of urgency.

Now what?

Where do I go from here?

Ellie was relieved when Taylor seized the initiative. She pulled out of range and sat back on her heels, straddling Ellie's hips and shrugged out of her top and bra, her full breasts with rose colored aureoles bobbing as she moved. Ellie envied Taylor's easy grace and her complete lack of self-consciousness about her naked body.

As if picking up on Ellie's thoughts, Taylor gave her a long searching look, her expression serious.

"Are you sure about this?"

Was she?

Faced with decision time, Ellie hesitated.

Would Taylor deride her naivety?

Would she freeze at the crucial moment, as she'd done so many times with Paul?

Ellie shuddered at the memory. Once Paul had realized that she wasn't going to orgasm no matter what he did, or how long he spent on foreplay, he'd given up trying and simply taken his own pleasure without any regard to her feelings.

No! She refused to dwell on her fears. This was a new beginning, with all thoughts of sexual ineptitude banished forever. Best let Taylor remain in control though.

She knew next to nothing about lesbian love or sex. Ellie sighed. What little knowledge she had, came from accidentally witnessing some of the more bizarre sexual practices that Sam and her procession of girl friends enjoyed. An icy shiver snaked down her spine—she would have to trust that Taylor wasn't into leather, whips, chains and lethal-looking spiky things.

Yes?

No?

Fear of the unknown sent a brief moment of terror flashing through Ellie's mind before her lips parted in a smile. "I'm sure...I want to know, to feel..."

Taylor returned her smile. "Okay, Ellie, I'll take things slowly and we'll stop if you're not comfortable."

Ellie nodded her mouth too dry to speak. Although she longed to scream out fuck me hard, fuck me now, no more foreplay, no holding back, she realized that she needed to take this really slowly, one step at a time—let Taylor teach her the secrets of lesbian love, what to do and how to enjoy sexual play so she might experience total fulfillment without any constraints. She sat up and tried to take off her top but Taylor pushed her back down.

"Let me do that." Without further ado, Taylor removed Ellie's top and bra so they were both naked from the waist up. Then she leant forward to claim a kiss. Ellie drew on a sharp intake of breath as her highly sensitized nipples brushed against Taylor's bare skin. Taylor broke contact and pulled back immediately.

"Don't stop." Ellie pulled Taylor's head down to her aching breasts, holding her firmly until she got the message and took one aching nipple into her mouth. Ellie relaxed, savoring the erotic pleasure as Taylor explored one hardened tip with her tongue and teeth. After a few minutes, she transferred her mouth to the other breast while her fingers plucked at the now wet nipple, driving Ellie into a frenzy of desire. She wriggled, desperately trying to grind her dripping pussy against Taylor's and not quite succeeding.

"Please, I want... I need...I need you to fuck me now." Ellie pleaded as flames licked at her already overheated core.

"Have patience." Taylor raised her head and gazed intently down upon Ellie. "Let's finish undressing first and then we'll see."

Subdued by her hot penetrating stare, Ellie meekly allowed Taylor to take full control of her body. Taylor's hands drifted down her thighs along with her skirt. She whimpered with pleasure at the feather light brush of fingertips against her sensitive skin. Her stockings followed next and then Taylor turned her attention to the black lace thong. She hooked her fingers into both sides and worked the damp scrap of fabric slowly downward until it cleared her feet.

Ellie gasped when she felt cool air kiss her heated pussy. She resisted the urge to wrap her arms about her body to cover her nakedness. Instead, she watched in awe as Taylor stood and casually shimmied out of her remaining clothes with uninhibited grace.

God she was beautiful. Ellie's gaze followed Taylor's movements sweeping down from her face over her sumptuous breasts to her slender waist then on to the neatly trimmed triangle of dark blonde hair at the apex of her thighs. She could smell Taylor's need, at least she assumed it was hers, maybe it was both of them combined—the intoxicating musky aroma made her ache to take control, to explore Taylor's body intimately, and experience the pleasure burying her face in her moist warmth.

Taylor pulled Ellie to her feet, backed her hard up against the wall and moved in to claim a hot kiss. She forced Ellie's lips apart and plundered the depths of her mouth until their tongues met in an erotic dance. Then Taylor cupped Ellie's ass, lifted her, and encouraged her to wrap her legs around her waist.

Waves of pure sensation raced through Ellie's body converging like flaming arrows deep inside her as their naked flesh fused together.

Oh God! She was on a high. Being with a man had never felt this good. Ellie ground harder, a pulse plucking urgent vibrations from her hot, wet crotch. Hotter, wetter and more urgent than ever before, tension increasing, gaining momentum like a giant tidal wave, yet being held back by a dam wall.

Taylor suddenly broke the kiss, her breathing ragged. "Wait!" She pulled away from the wall with Ellie still held tightly to her. "Not here. We'll be more comfortable in the bedroom."

Without waiting for a response, Taylor carried Ellie into the bedroom, dropped her onto the bed then slid alongside her with their bodies barely touching. After a few seconds, Taylor trailed her fingers lightly across Ellie's throat, just skimming her collarbone letting each leisurely sweep travel a little further until she reached her breasts. Ellie whimpered, and pushed against Taylor's hand encouraging her to tease her aching nipples harder. Spikes of pleasure clawed at Ellie. She wanted to scream. Taylor leant closer, their lips barely touching, and whispered against Ellie's mouth.

"Let me love you."

A tingle of anticipation rippled through Ellie's body. "Please." She expressed her plea on a breathy sigh.

Taylor needed no further invitation. She sealed her lips to Ellie's, invading her mouth by force. Breath hot and heavy with the scent of arousal, tongues entwined, they thrashed against each other, arms and legs entangled in a frantic effort to get maximum skin on skin contact.

Ellie's head swam, unable to keep pace with all the new sensations bombarding her. Then Taylor slid one hand between her trembling thighs, dipped her fingers into her juices and spread them to her clit. She rolled the throbbing bud between her fingers.

Jeez!

Violent shockwaves reverberated through her body, and she marveled how good it felt, how wet and hot Taylor made her. At that point Ellie lost all vestige of control. She gave herself up to the moment and let her instinct take over. Her hands roamed Taylor's body, exploring, reveling in the feel of satiny skin and soft curves that complemented the firmness of muscles. Then Ellie grew bolder, parting Taylor's labia and seeking her silky moisture.

Within seconds, Taylor shuddered and spasmed around her finger, her muscles pulsing, the contractions pulling Ellie deeper into the hot cavity.

Taylor gave a soft growl and rolled Ellie under her. Then she rained hot kisses down Ellie's throat to her breasts and more slowly on down to the searing heat between her thighs. "Aaah!" Ellie arched her back, thrusting her hips off the mattress, her body trembling against the assault of Taylor's mouth. Then Taylor pushed her thighs up and wide apart, opening her fully to her tongue.

A pulse roared in Ellie's ears, she couldn't think straight. Her body bucked against Taylor as if had a life of its own. Waves of sensation swept through her body. Taylor's tongue probed her pussy then withdrew to sweep across her clit before returning to her slit.

"Fuck me, please…I need relief," Ellie pleaded. Then a very familiar tension gripped her body, her muscles clenched in response, leaving her poised on the brink of the elusive orgasm yet resisting that final leap into the void.

Taylor responded. She tongue fucked Ellie, deep, hard, and fast. Then she withdrew to tease Ellie with gentle sweeps of her tongue across the ultra sensitive flesh, finally curling her tongue around

Ellie's clit and taking the throbbing mass into her mouth. Ellie screamed. Her finger nails driving into Taylor's scalp as she tore at her hair. Her body racked with an incredible pain as the longed for orgasm shattered the invisible dam wall and ripped her apart. Taylor moved swiftly back to Ellie's slit her tongue picking up the rhythm of Ellie's body as it pumped a never-ending stream of scalding liquid into her core.

"Oh!" Ellie gasped. She was floating on air. Her body alive with delicious tingles radiating out from her core to every nerve ending. Taylor brought her down slowly, kissing her way back up Ellie's body then holding her close until she stilled and her breathing returned to near normal.

When their lips met, Ellie tasted herself on Taylor's lips and tongue. Erotically enticing both sweet and salty at the same time, not a bit as she'd imagined. Her mouth watered. She could only imagine what it would be like to taste Taylor, to dip her tongue into her honey and suck her dry. Just thinking about it got her juices flowing again.

Ellie snuggled into Taylor's arms, contented. "I never knew…I…Is it always so…?" Words failed her.

Taylor held Ellie away from her and frowned. "Was that your first orgasm?"

"Yes." The admission brought a rush of heat to Ellie's cheeks. "Twenty-eight, and still an orgasmic virgin."

"Then you have a lot of catching up to do." Taylor chuckled softly. "Think of what you've just experienced as the aperitif at the beginning of a banquet. Trust me, it gets a whole lot better when you progress to the main course and desert."

"Mmmm!" Ellie giggled. "In that case, since you know how much I love my food. I think I'm about ready for the next course now."

ALL FOR LOVE

"What do you mean, you're not going... Why not?" I glanced up from the tickets in my hand and my heart sank. Cheryl's implacable stance promised a confrontation that I could well do without after a long day in the courtroom attempting to defend the indefensible. On days like today I'm apt to question my sanity in opting for a career in public defense rather than accepting the lucrative offer I'd received from a private law practice. The answer, however, always comes down to why I chose the law in the first place. It does not matter how difficult or hopeless the case. I believe in, and strive for, a fair and level playing field for everybody regardless of their income or status.

"Because..." Cheryl didn't bother to elaborate but merely glared.

"What's changed? You were all for going to this event when we put our names into the draw for tonight's special showing." Acutely aware of Cheryl's volatility, I tried to keep my tone neutral although uncertainty as to how she might react to the question had already tied my stomach into a tight knot.

Where had my beautiful, vivacious, lover gone? What had happened to change her into this surly imposter, who bore no resemblance to the angel I'd set my heart on marrying from the day she walked into my life with her bright smile and easy wit? Compassion melted my heart. I wanted to take her in my arms. Hold her tight, and comfort her. To soothe away the hurt she clearly carried with her everywhere like a heavy burden, if only I knew what it was, but I didn't. How could I begin to understand, when she'd hardly spoken a word for weeks now, let alone confided her darkest secrets or her fears?

"Was I?" Cheryl's tone conveyed total surprise at the mention of this hitherto eagerly anticipated social event. "Lighten up, Tara. You're doing my head in with your constant carping about this stupid show!"

"*Lighten up…*" Barely holding onto my temper, I echoed her scathing riposte. "Is that all you have to say? May I remind you that you were the one who begged me to put our names into the draw for these tickets. Because, and I quote, "Lee Delahaye is my inspiration" and "I'd be so stoked to have the once in a lifetime opportunity to see the retrospective of her formative body art alongside all her regular artwork." Oh, yes, I almost forgot to mention that this event supports our favorite LGBT charity."

"Did I say all that?" Cheryl shrugged, avoiding my gaze as she raked paint-stained fingers through her short brown hair. "I honestly can't remember."

Clearly braless, her breasts thrust against her shirt as she expelled a ragged breath. My body pulsed with a need that demanded instant satisfaction as I fought the overwhelming urge to rip the fabric apart and feast upon the sweetness below. I clenched my fists, and drove my fingernails deep into my palms, in an attempt to stop myself from reaching for her when I knew that doing so would only drive her further away. I'd finally given up trying to love or comfort her, since every time I got close to her now she rejected me. It hadn't always been like this but I couldn't fathom out where or why everything had gone so horribly wrong.

"Do you know, or even care, how much these fucking tickets cost me?" I felt the sharp sting of my accusation and immediately wished the words unsaid. A dark red stain spread across Cheryl's pale cheeks, almost as if I'd physically slapped her. Regret escaped from my lips in a long drawn sigh. This sniping back and forth was getting us nowhere fast. I wish I knew how to break the cycle but that was like wishing for the moon. My failure to find the elusive solution to our current problems left me feeling totally inadequate. Hell, I was the strong one in this relationship; I ought to be able to put things right.

"No, I don't..." For what seemed an eternity, Cheryl just stared blankly at me, as if she had no idea who I was then she turned away and stomped across the hall. "Take somebody else or sell them if you're that concerned about the money but count me out." She barely broke her stride to fling the final caustic rebuff over her shoulder and then punctuated her words with a thunderous slam of the bedroom door.

I resisted the urge to follow in search of an explanation. Experience had taught me no good would come from doing so. Cheryl wasn't in any mood to listen to reason. I glanced down at the gilt-edged, engraved pasteboard still grasped in my hand, shook my head, and tossed the tickets into the trash. I couldn't bear to worry about them, or the two thousand dollars they had cost me, when my main concern was Cheryl. This episode typified her strange behavior – up one minute, down the next.

Since this crazy situation began, I'd given her my unconditional love and support only to have it tossed right back into my face on every occasion. Whatever the nature of the problem that was screwing up her mind, it had sent everything we'd built together over five years crashing onto the rocks until there was hardly a thing left worth saving.

Much as I hate to admit failure, I'd reached the point where I really couldn't take any more. Cheryl had just fucked up her last chance to fix things between us. Tonight's tantrum proved, if any further proof were needed, that there was nothing left of our relationship but an empty shell. I brushed stinging tears of regret from my eyes. Right now I needed to get out of the apartment, and away from Cheryl, before she dragged me down with her. We both needed some breathing space. Maybe a few days apart would bring Cheryl to her senses, or at least resolve the situation one way or the other. I grabbed my cell phone and texted Ariadne, a long-time friend and colleague, to beg a bed for the night then went to pack a bag.

On my way across the bedroom with an armful of underwear, I stopped dead, diverted from my task by the sight of Cheryl's naked body through the semi-opaque shower screen in the en suite. Her pose, with head thrown back and ample breasts thrust forward, nipples standing proud from rosy-pink aureoles, was incredibly sexy. Hot juices flooded my pussy at the sight of water cascading over that gorgeous body. A body I hadn't touched in months, since her first step had been to slam the door on any intimacy.

Desire overtook common sense when I saw those water droplets caressing all the places my lips and tongue remembered. My mind conjured up a raft of sensual images which in turn led to us enjoying one last fuck, just for old time's sake.

Jeez! How sick is that?

The thought had barely left my head before my libido seized control, as it always did when I was around her naked body. I kicked off my shoes, shed my formal business suit, and shimmied out of my under garments in the few seconds it took to cross the bedroom then I pushed aside the screen and joined Cheryl under the spray.

"No, Tara. Please don't… You mustn't…"

Cheryl's half-hearted attempt to push me away merely increased my desire. I slammed her hard against the tiled wall and trailed hungry kisses down her throat. Our slick bodies melded breast to breast, in familiar harmony as I sucked and nibbled the soft flesh below her ear like a starving woman – which indeed I was. I hadn't realized how horny I was until this moment presented itself.

My hands moved lower to cup her ass and ease her closer. I rotated my hips to bring my shaven mound in better contact with hers and immediately red-hot fingers of sensation raked at my body. It felt so good, so right, to have her naked body tight against me and I intended to make the most of what might be our final time together. I thrust against her, savoring the pulses of my arousal, searching for the elusive pinnacle of satisfaction.

I forced myself to take things slowly, hoping that by doing so Cheryl would respond. Much as I'd expected, she remained totally impassive to the touch of my lips and my hands, although she made no further move to stop me, which, I suppose, counted as a victory of sorts. I kissed my way down her neck then back up again my pussy throbbing with unfulfilled need. I wanted her so badly pain tore at every nerve ending.

When I grew too impatient to hold back, I snaked one hand between Cheryl's thighs. Her clit immediately swelled and hardened under my touch, and the hungry beast inside me morphed into a starving monster. My water-slick fingers slid back and forth, teasing her, feeling her, seeking entry to her tightly closed slit.

"Open for me." I used one knee to move her legs wider apart and then drilled two fingers deep inside her. My hunger drove me on. I dipped my head lower and used my teeth to graze one of her nipples while I pumped my hand.

Cheryl moaned softly. The sound of her arousal resonated from deep down in her throat like a feline purr. Then she suddenly came alive and began to grind agitatedly against my thrusting fingers. "Oh, Tara I'm…" She shuddered into silence, grabbed a handful of my hair and yanked my head back and then reached down to kiss me, forcing my lips apart as she plunged her tongue into my mouth.

My tongue intertwined with hers before thrusting into her mouth to match the rhythm of my hand. I felt a faint fluttering in her thighs then, within seconds, her whole body began to shake violently. Fueled by the frenzy of her approaching climax I drove my fingers into her, harder, faster, deeper, my own arousal heightened by the action of our slick bodies moving in unison.

We came together. My own climax coursed through my body like a wildfire, robbing me of both breath and strength. Vibrant crimson flames blazed behind my closed eyelids, and the roar of crashing waves filled my ears only to be overshadowed by Cheryl's scream as it rent the air and echoed off the tiled walls. Her internal muscles trapped my hand in a vice-like grip as an intense orgasm took control of her body.

Still shaking violently, she collapsed onto the shower floor taking me down with her. After a few moments, I reached up and cut the spray then held her tight until all vestiges of the trembling ceased and her ragged breathing returned to near normal. Then I wrapped her in a large towel, carried her through to the bedroom, and laid her gently on our bed.

For a long time we clung to each other, in total silence, just sharing kisses and the intimate togetherness that had been missing from our relationship for so long.

Irrationally, I wanted this night to go on forever so we'd never again have to face the hurt and loneliness of these past few months. However, I knew deep down in my heart, that unless some miracle happened, there was no reprieve. Come tomorrow morning I'd have to face the world knowing our relationship was dead.

After a while, I began to stroke her neck, making each sweep of my fingers longer until finally I parted the towel to reveal her breasts, which seemed much fuller than I remembered. Cheryl groaned when I leant forward and took one succulent nipple between my lips. I teased the tip with my tongue while my fingers carefully spread the remaining folds of the towel so every part of her was exposed for my pleasure.

My heart overflowed with love and tenderness as I drew back and gazed down at my angel. In all our five years together, I don't believe she had ever looked as beautiful as she did at this moment. Anticipation sent my pulse rocketing into orbit and my pussy filled with hot juices as fresh tingles of animal lust surged through my body. I trailed my fingers over her silky skin, my lips following the same path, caressing all those secret places I knew she loved me to touch until she begged me with her groans and wild thrashing movements to take her again.

Happy to oblige, I parted her thighs and leant forward to sweep my tongue slowly over her slit, lapping the honey sweet juices now flowing freely from her pussy. She smelt absolutely divine, a subtle aroma of sexual arousal mixed with a soft floral fragrance that was all her own.

"Tara! Please...I can't..." Her voice cracked. She bucked wildly against my mouth, and her nails raked across my scalp as she scrabbled for purchase. This was more like my Cheryl, my fabulous lover – eager, sensuous and oh so fuckable.

I pushed her legs up, and she opened for me like the delicate petals of a tropical flower to a humming bird. And, like a bird, I buried my tongue deep inside her, feeling her muscles pull me further into her pulsating depths as I teased her swollen clit with my finger. Within seconds, she exploded onto my tongue in a rush of sweet honey, her breath coming in harsh gasps and her body racked with spasms.

I kissed my way slowly back up her body until we were face to face. Her eyes glowed with a contentment that I hadn't witnessed in ages. I smiled, eased her closer to me and felt her relax in my arms. Maybe all she'd needed was a good fuck to set her right.

I had almost fallen into a post coital sleep when Cheryl's long drawn sigh pulled me awake. I drew back and searched her face. "Are you going to tell me what's bothering you?"

Cheryl shook her head and avoided my gaze.

"Come on… surely whatever is bothering you isn't so awful that you can't share it with me." I cupped her face in my hands and kissed her softly. "I love you. You're my whole world. If something hurts you it hurts me, too."

For several agonizing seconds she remained immobile and silent. I thought she'd shut me out again, but finally she threw off her torpor to look directly at me, her eyes deeply troubled, and her face drawn. "I'm pregnant."

I stared at her, dumbfounded by her revelation, yet delighted she'd realized her dream. I knew how much she longed for a baby. We'd already explored every avenue and, as far as I was aware, had yet to decide between IVF, with all the attendant counseling and red tape, or a signing up to a private sperm donor service for a DIY conception.

"How? When?" I frowned. Why hadn't I known about it or been involved in her decision and the actual procedure like we'd discussed?

"There! I knew you'd react like that." She scooted away from me, retreating to the far side of our large bed. She leant against the wall, pulled her knees up to her chin and wrapped her arms around them. Tears welled up in her eyes.

"If you must know I screwed a man!"

I sensed there was more to come and her antagonistic glower warned me not to respond in haste.

"Before you ask, no, I don't know his real name, or anything else about him...he was just some guy I met in a hotel bar. He was staying there for a couple of nights and looking for a lay."

"Oh God, Cheryl! When did...?" My heart went out to her. I'd always known she hated the idea of a clinical conception but I never thought she'd become so desperate, so mad, as to screw a man, a total stranger, in the slim hope of conceiving naturally.

"Last time you went to New York. I knew it was the right time in my cycle, and I just went out on the pull."

Cheryl's defiant tone made her actions sound so calculating, and sordid, but I knew her and was certain it hadn't really been like that. I counted backwards. Just under four months, about the time she fell into this strange mood. This changed everything. Excitement bubbled up in my throat almost choking me. We were going to be parents in a little over five months from now and I wanted to share in every single moment of the journey with her.

"Come here." I opened my arms. I couldn't feel jealousy, or anger, nor condemn her for wanting the joy of motherhood, but to risk her life for her dream was something else.

She gave me a hostile glare, but didn't move. "It's all right, you're quite safe. I didn't catch anything. I got the results of my tests this week and they all came back negative."

"Did I say anything?" She must have read my mind and misunderstood my concern for her welfare.

"You didn't need to…I saw the disgust written on your face and believe me, it matched everything I've felt of myself f…for using him and what I did to you… For betraying you like that." She dissolved into tears, her anguished outpouring transmitting vibrations through her entire body like the ever widening aftershocks of an earthquake.

"You haven't betrayed me, I love you and I'm so happy you're pregnant." I shot across the bed, took her into my arms and stroked her hair until her sobs subsided.

"Really?" Cheryl sniffed and tipped her face up to look me in the eye seeking reassurance.

"Yes… really. This is our future… I want to be a part of it, to share your hopes and fears in equal measure, and that naturally includes everything you know about the biological father of our baby so I can picture him and understand what made you take such an enormous risk."

"I'm not totally insane." Cheryl expelled a long jerky breath and scrubbed at her eyes. "I chose a good hotel, the Maple Court, and he seemed quite respectable, well-spoken and well educated. Not bad looking for a guy; tall, dark and handsome, a bit like you."

She attempted a smile, but didn't quite pull it off then she bit down on a quivering bottom lip and lowered her gaze.

"He bought me three champagne cocktails and talked endlessly about his family. He even showed me their pictures – beautiful twin girls, the image of their mother, with baby-blonde curls and angelic blue eyes, and a boy about four with his dark hair and eyes. I nearly backed out when he told me his wife was expecting again, but then I reckoned that it was a good omen and it proved he'd got the necessary ammunition, so I played along with his little charade of "I'm not actually cheating on my wife, if I tell you about her" and concentrated hard on the real reason why I was there. To give him credit, he did treat me to dinner in the restaurant – although I can't tell you what we ate, it's all a blur, then we went up to his suite and..."

Cheryl made it all sound so simplistic, so cut and dried. Yet, reading between the lines, I was certain she must have been terrified something would go horribly wrong and there was one point that puzzled me. "How the hell did you manage to get him to do it without a condom?"

"I got him all hot and horny before I told him I was allergic to condoms, by that time he was too far gone to worry whether I might get pregnant, or anything else.

"The sex was horrible I almost gagged when he…" Cheryl shuddered against my chest. "Mercifully it was over very quickly. I actually felt him come inside me, just a few spurts of hot liquid, and you've got no idea how hard I prayed that my sacrifice hadn't been in vain. It wasn't, it worked, I'm pregnant and…" She sucked in a ragged breath. "Are you sure you're ready for this…I'm…we're expecting twins."

I gulped back tears of joy and hugged her tightly. The news just got better and better. A couple of hours ago I'd all but given up hope that we could salvage our relationship, and now it appeared we might have a future again.

Would that future extend to marriage?

Cheryl must know I'd always wanted her to be my wife. Hell, of course she knew, I proposed to her with monotonous regularity, every Christmas, birthday and of course our anniversary. She had always refused until earlier this year when, to stop me making a total exhibition of myself in the fancy restaurant to which I'd taken her to celebrate our fifth anniversary, she'd finally caved in and promised me that if she ever became pregnant she would marry me so our baby arrived in the world with legally married parents. I wanted that more than ever now, even if we were forced to move away from California in order to marry.

I wasn't particularly concerned where we lived, providing I had Cheryl by my side for the rest of our natural lives – Massachusetts, Connecticut, Canada, or even somewhere overseas, the only criteria being wherever we settled must not only recognize same-sex marriage but give us equal status with heterosexual couples. No half measures, when we got married; I wanted to give my beautiful bride everything she deserved.

Now I hesitated to put her promise to the test. What if she said no? My heart sank at the thought of another rejection. Maybe tonight wasn't the best time to raise the topic. Besides, I could think of better ways to cement our renewed relationship. No! I forced myself to ignore the demands of my libido and my throbbing pussy and concentrate on Cheryl.

"Twins! That's the best news. I'm so happy for you…for us…Although I can't believe you kept all this to yourself." I held her at arm's length and scanned her face. "Why on earth didn't you tell me before?"

Cheryl shook her head. "I suppose I needed time to work through all the consequences by myself and then get used to the idea of being pregnant. I suppose I really didn't believe it had happened, until I got the print of the scan. Anyway, I didn't think you'd understand."

"Why ever not…" I shook my head. "Don't you trust me? Jeez, Cheryl, we've been together over five years, surely we're close enough to share something this important – something that affects us both."

"Yes, Tara, but…"

"But nothing, Cheryl." Her constant uncertainty stretched my patience. "Do I come across as a selfish bitch that wouldn't stand by you at the very time you needed me most?"

"No… Of course not."

I watched a tangle of emotions chase across her drawn face and wished there was a way to convince Cheryl to trust me – I knew trust was the single aspect of our relationship that she found particularly difficult. Her previous partner had treated her very badly and it had taken me months to persuade her I wasn't about to do the same. I thought we'd finally cleared that hurdle and put the past behind us but now, it appeared, we were back to square one.

I took a deep breath, trying to lift the heavy band of sadness constricting my chest. I didn't know if I could cope with starting over, when what we'd had up until recently had been so good in every way. Fantastic sex, love, laughter, and being there for each other no matter what, not to mention a full social life filled with fun and good friends. Although, when I came to think of it, since we stopped socializing the invitations had dried up and our friends had quit calling.

Hell, no! Somehow, I knew I'd find a way to turn this around and finally persuade Cheryl to marry me, to make that binding commitment to me and to our children. We belonged together like strawberries and cream. I wanted us to grow old together, and make more memories than would fill a thousand albums. I'd pledged myself to her and our partnership five years ago, and now I was even more determined to convince her to do the same.

"Then prove it… Prove that you both trust and love me, and that you're committed to our relationship. Marry me, like you promised."

Cheryl pulled away from me, her sharp intake of breath sounding like the steam vent on a pressure pipe. My heart sank at the shell-shocked expression on her face. Her mouth opened and closed but the anticipated refusal failed to materialize, she just sat there immobile whilst I cursed myself for forcing the issue. I should never have pushed her to make such a major decision when she was so emotionally fragile. This wasn't the right time but, in truth, there never would be a right time in Cheryl's case. She spent her whole life imprisoned from reality by a perpetual fear of commitment. I just had to discover some way to breach the walls, and then find the key to unlock the cage surrounding her heart.

I'd done it before so repeating the process should be easy, shouldn't it?

* * * *

Six months later, I stood on the patio of our lovely new home on the outskirts of Boston and thanked the Lord for my blessings. I'd just married the most wonderful woman on earth, and life couldn't get any better. Cheryl's irrepressible laughter floated across the garden that, just for today to celebrate our wedding, had been transformed into a fairyland of white and silver by our friends.

I scanned the assembled guests for my new wife and soon spotted Cheryl chatting with our witnesses, Hayden and Dee, just outside the gazebo where the ceremony had taken place earlier. Surprisingly, given our track record, everything had run smoothly although, standing waiting for Cheryl to arrive for the ceremony, I'd been on tenterhooks that something would go wrong, until the first notes of Händel's organ voluntary, *Arrival of the Queen of Sheba*, filled the silence. I'd turned for a first glimpse of my lovely bride walking towards me along the rose strewn path, with Dee and Hayden bringing up the rear carrying a twin each. My breath caught in my throat. Cheryl looked absolutely radiant in her wedding dress, a mid-calf sheath in delicate pastel shades, like a fading rainbow, overlaid with filmy white chiffon. It had proved the perfect choice for both her figure and coloring. It was so good to see her relaxed and enjoying life again after all the trauma of these past months. I hurried across the grass to her side and kissed her, tasting the sweetness of wine on her lips. "Enjoying yourself?"

"Mmmm." Cheryl returned my kiss. Her hand strayed down my back to cup my ass and ease me closer. Her warm breath fanned my cheek as she whispered in my ear. "I plan to enjoy tonight even more."

"I can hardly wait." I slipped one hand between us to caress her mound and felt a shiver ripple through her gorgeous body. Hot steel fingers raked my pussy into throbbing awareness as I contemplated the delights that lay ahead, once I got her alone, naked, and begging me to fuck her in all the ways she loved best. I clenched my thighs together to stem the wetness seeping through my thong.

Cheryl sighed and pushed into my hand. "Even better, Hayden and Dee have offered to take the babies with them so we can have a proper wedding night with no interruptions for feeds and such like."

I blessed our friends for their thoughtfulness. Why hadn't I thought of that? The twin's early arrival into the world, at seven months, had disrupted our original wedding plans. It had taken us another two months to get our two little angels, Alicia and Megan, home from NICU and then a further month to organize our big day.

I turned toward Hayden and Dee, a smile on my lips. "Thank you." I drew both women close in a group hug. "I owe you big time for this."

"We'll hold you to that," Hayden said, as she exchanged a questioning look with Dee and got a nod in response. "We have some news too but it'll wait until after your honeymoon..."

"You can't stop there. Tell all," Cheryl chimed into the pause in her usual forthright manner.

Hayden shrugged. "Okay, if you insist... only this is your special day and we didn't want to steal your thunder. We've decided to take a leaf out of your book and tie the knot before our own little bundle of joy arrives in September and..."

"Holy cow!" Cheryl's squeal was loud enough to wake the dead but, for good measure, she also clapped her hands together to ensure she had everybody's attention. "Listen up, everyone, Hayden and Dee are getting married!" I wasn't surprised that she'd wasted no time before broadcasting the news. I eased out of the melee when she launched into a round of enthusiastic hugs and kisses, with all the guests who'd gathered around to toast the happy couple and fire questions at them. All this excitement was too much for me to stomach.

Much as I enjoyed our friends' company, I couldn't help but wish all our guests gone so that we might be alone for a private celebration of our union

A couple of hours later, my wish was granted. Hayden and Dee were the last to leave. Cheryl gripped my hand, her nails digging into my flesh, as we watched her Dodge drive away with our two precious bundles snug in their special car seats, and my heart sank when I detected a film of tears misting her eyes as we turned to enter the house. Maybe letting Hayden and Dee take Alicia and Megan away for the night wasn't such a good idea after all.

I needn't have worried. Within seconds of kicking the front door closed with her heel, Cheryl pinned me against the wood, her breath hot on my skin as she rained kisses down my throat. The pulsating fire in my pussy ratcheted up my breathing until I was gasping for air. I thrust against Cheryl, my hands molding her curves. The need to fuck her until we

were both sated nearly drove me insane. "Not here."
I pushed away from the door, grabbed Cheryl by the
hand, and pulled her down the hall.

We barely got inside our bedroom before she
started to strip me. "Come on!" she growled as her
fingers scrabbled at the buttons on my shirt until the
fabric parted. She pushed the shirt down my arms
and let it fall to the floor. Her eager lips sought my
breast, sucking greedily at one pert nipple through
the fine cotton, while her hands worked to free the
zipper on my slacks. Cheryl dropped to her knees in
front of me, her hands gliding down my legs along
with the fabric.

I groaned as she pressed her mouth to my damp
thong and almost came apart right then, so strong
were the pulses that clawed at my overheated pussy.
Her soft hands caressed my thighs as they slid back
up to cup my ass and hold my now trembling body to
her lips. I fisted my hands in her hair and bit down on
my lip, trying not to lose control.

Cheryl pushed me back onto the bed with my feet
still on the floor and her fingers twisted in my thong.
The flimsy fabric required no more than a swift tug on
her part to tear and fall clear of my body. I spread my
legs and lifted my ass to welcome her fingers as they
plunged deep inside my slit.

"Fuck me. Please… I need to come." I bucked wildly against her until she responded and began to pump hard, her fingers moving easily in my slick channel. When she drew my clit into her mouth and teased it with her tongue I couldn't hold back any longer.

I screamed my relief as the world exploded, rocking and crashing my body in a never-ending whirlpool of emotion.

"Wow!" Cheryl sat back on her heels and gazed at me, laughter sparkling in her eyes. "When you come, you sure do it in style."

I smiled through my tears, unable to move or speak.

Cheryl stood and moved to the center of the room where she struck a sexy pose. Then she reached around and worked the zipper slowly down her back before she shimmied out of her dress, leaving it pooled on the floor around her feet. I almost jumped her then, she looked so fuckable wearing nothing but her spiked heels, a lacy white chemise with suspenders and stockings, and matching thong. My body hummed with anticipation as she stepped out of her shoes, then unclipped each stocking in turn, sliding it down her legs and off her pretty feet like she was performing an exotic striptease. The chemise went next, revealing her sumptuous breasts with soft rosy aureoles and prominent nipples that I ached to suckle. Finally, she smoothed her hands over her neat waist and flat stomach, then she hooked her fingers into the thong and worked it slowly down her thighs until the scrap of fabric dropped to the floor so she could step out of it.

She was so beautiful. I could never get enough of her body.

"Come here." I smiled as Cheryl fell into my open arms, her naked body melding with mine, ready to start a whole new chapter in our lives

WEATHERING THE STORM

Rain beat relentlessly against the window and a rumble of thunder reverberated in the distance. I hesitated in the lobby of the building where I leased a small office, debating my next move. The prospect of staying in town for however long it took the storm to pass thrilled me nearly as much as an hour-long drive home along a highway which always flooded during heavy rain. I scanned the sky for the inevitable streak of lightning that would make the decision for me.

"Oh, no, I don't believe this rain!"

The woman's voice sounded very close I glanced around and instantly my heart jolted in my chest. The quip about us needing a boat to get out of here froze on my lips. For the first time, the object of my unattainable desire stood close enough for me to touch her and to inhale her subtle, floral fragrance.

Seen close up she was sexier than I could possibly have imagined. My nipples - never slow in coming forward—peaked in instant awareness at her proximity, followed quickly by similar reactions from the rest of my body. Sad to say I couldn't remember when I last enjoyed this urgent rush of moist heat or the uncontrollable spasms deep inside my pussy. I clenched my thighs and savored the moment, welcoming the waves of exquisite pleasure sweeping over me.

A jagged flash of bright lightning chased away another clap of thunder. Her eyes widened and a small scream escaped her lips.

So she's frightened of electric storms.

I clutched at the tiny scrap of information like a starving woman unexpectedly finding a box of food waiting on her doorstep. My arms ached to wrap her tight, to protect her from fear, but I couldn't take that liberty when didn't know her name or anything else about her other than what I'd seen from afar, or could imagine.

And my imagination is pretty inventive at times.

For two long months, I've found myself captivated by this sexy wench. Ever since she began work as a receptionist for a recruitment agency in the glass-fronted office right across the corridor from mine.

A few times I've been tempted to waylay her in the communal restroom or wander over to enquire about job opportunities for graphic designers but always stopped myself from doing something so crass or so blatantly obvious. Nevertheless, I kept my options open always ready to exploit a valid excuse to speak to her if one came my way. I watched her avidly each day and marveled at the many different outfits she possessed. Clothes that revealed intoxicating glimpses of the gorgeous body underneath them, plus flashes of her splendid thighs displayed to best advantage by the miniskirts she favored.

God how I fancy her.

No! Too tame, I swore silently, angry with the sudden inability to express myself.

I want to slam her up against the wall, rip the clothes from her body with my teeth then wrap those long legs around my waist and fuck her until we're both sated.

At around twenty-one or two, she's a lot younger than my forty-three years.

Far too young for me.

Willow tall, she matches me for height, her slim waist and firm breasts make me envious of her youth. A silky cap of burnished gold hair frames her heart-shaped face and just brushes her cheeks when she moves. Long dark lashes shade cobalt blue eyes that sparkle like multi-faceted sapphires when her soft rosy lips part in a smile.

Oh, how those lips beg me to kiss them.

I know I shouldn't contemplate such things. I'm way past the age to have a teenage crush, or succumb to the lure of a sexy young femme who ordinarily wouldn't give me a second glance. Why would this lovely creature be interested in a woman with graying hair and wrinkles? Although I'm a fairly athletic build, with not an ounce of fat to spare, I have to face one unpalatable fact, I'm old enough to be her mother.

Yet I couldn't stop watching, or dreaming of what might be, even though I believed she was as far out of my reach as the stars. While I wanted to trust my gaydar, I feared it wasn't giving me reliable signals where she's concerned. For I'd also seen her in the arms of a young man, laughing, kissing, and going off together at the end of the day. The image of them naked, limbs entwined in the throes of passion, tortured me in the depths of the night.

"I think we're going to get very wet." Her soft voice, with just the hint of a southern drawl, tugged me back to the present.

Wet!

Oh, yes! I'm already wet just thinking of the games we might play if I kidnapped her and carried her home tonight. I can see us clearly, in my imagination, swimming together in my outdoor pool. Our naked bodies caressed by silky fingers of warm water. Kissing, touching, teasing and then, unable to wait another minute, making out on the poolside under a starry sky before moving indoors to share a shower. With warm spray and softly perfumed lotions to create an atmosphere of sensuality in which anything is possible, I can think of so many ways I'd love to pleasure her with my tongue and hands. Later, after we finished the bottle of champagne I've been keeping for just this occasion, we'd probably raid my big toy box. The image of her sitting astride my hips riding the strapless double, those gorgeous breasts bouncing and her fingers tearing at her clit as she approaches her climax, sends fresh pulses of energy to my core. The urge to touch myself and relieve the pressure is almost too much to bear.

Hey, down girl! You're in a public place.

I pushed the erotic images firmly from my mind. Since I hadn't used those toys in ages, preferring to pleasure myself with my hands and the one favorite vibrator that I always keep under my pillow, I was probably overreacting.

"You may be right." I returned her smile then tore my gaze from her luscious lips before I did something unforgivable. Outside, the curtain of rain distorted the flashing neon sign above the Italian restaurant a few yards away across the square. So close, I can almost smell fragrant espresso coffee mingling with the savory aroma of Dino's famous pasta dishes.

I'm tempted to ask her to share supper and a bottle of wine with me but hold my tongue, afraid to hear the unbearable rejection. My thoughts seesaw back and forth. This may be my only chance to spend some time in her company, to learn her name and a little about her. To have something tangible to feed on when I'm away from her.

Today she's wearing a low cut tunic, the soft blue matches her eyes perfectly. To make matters worse she's also showing enough cleavage to try the resolve of a saint, let alone a starving dyke whose imagination is way too vivid for her own peace of mind.

Nothing ventured, nothing gained. *I'll take my chance and ask her to join me. What have I got to lose?*

Everything.

A rabble of butterflies began a lively jig in my stomach reinforcing my reluctance to risk all by stepping into the unknown. I captured my bottom lip between my teeth. Fear of failure and the consequent disappointment constricted my throat making speech nigh on impossible.

Coward!

The accusation reverberated inside my head. The thought of what I might miss by not pursuing this chance sends shivers cascading down my spine. Chastened, I took a deep calming breath and open my mouth to speak.

"I wonder if…" she forestalled me before I could force the words out then she paused and shook her head.

What?

Something in her uncertain manner made my heart beat faster.

She fixed me with those gorgeous blue eyes. "Will you have a drink with me?" A faint blush swept across her cheeks and she dropped her gaze.

Did I hear her right?

My heart faltered momentarily and then raced away to compensate. Unbelievably, she'd taken the words right out of my mouth. I took a welcome breath. "Yes…I'd love to have a drink with you. Maybe we could have supper too?"

I glanced outside trying to judge how wet we might get in the short distance to Dino's. Although the rain had eased a little it still bounced off the ornamental paving separating us from the restaurant. I turned back to her and smiled. "Shall we brave the storm?"

She nodded agreement. It seemed the most natural thing in the world to hold out my hand to her and for her to take it. Hand in hand we ran across the square and into the steamy warmth of Dino's where, as if by prior arrangement, we headed straight for one of the high-walled booths in the back.

Being the perfect butch I got her seated first then slid in beside her. "Whew!" I shook the rain from my hair then turned eagerly to my companion. "I'm Laura Fenwick; I work in the office opposite you."

Dammit!

Why am I gabbling like an awkward teen on her first date?

Her eyes twinkled to match her smile. "Yes, I know...I've..." She paused when Rosa, Dino's pretty daughter, arrived to take our order. We quickly agreed on a bottle of Valpolicella and Fusilli alla Burina, Dino's signature dish of pasta served with sliced pork sausage cooked in wine, peas and a rich tomato sauce. She waited until Rosa was out of earshot before continuing softly. "I've watched you watching me. You have no idea how often I've willed you to come across so we could meet properly."

Really!

She'd watched me too!

Why hadn't I realized?

The thought that we'd wasted so much time rendered me speechless.

"It's nice to meet you at last, Laura, I'm Freya Johansen." Without warning, she leant across to kiss me full on the lips and my world exploded. That brief brush of her lips against mine took my breath away and unleashed a kaleidoscope of unimaginable sensations.

It took me several seconds before I finally managed to gather my scattered wits and sufficient breath to respond. "Hello Freya...I love your name, it suits you." Lured by her tantalizing perfume, I eased across the bench, closing the space between us and trapping her against the wall.

"Thank you." Her hand moved to cover mine where it rested on the green and white checked tablecloth and a fresh charge of electricity shot through my body.

Rosa arrived back with our wine before we'd exchanged more than a few breathless words. She set the glasses down, poured the wine, leaving the bottle on the table then lit the candles, and gave us a knowing wink before departing.

Freya glanced at the candles and burst out laughing. "Oh dear." She dabbed at her eyes with a tissue. "It seems Rosa is under the impression we're on a romantic date. Goodness knows what she's thinking about me now, as she did the same thing when I brought Davin, my little brother, in here the last time he came to town."

Her brother?

My heart skipped a beat.

Was that who I'd seen Freya kissing?

Possibly... Thinking back the kiss I'd witnessed might easily have been platonic rather than lover-like. Their youthful joy at being reunited combined with my innate jealousy had built it into something more.

I wanted to ask, but the question felt too personal, too much like declaring my feelings and I didn't want to scare her away. I was sure that she'd get around to telling me about a boyfriend, if there was one, in her own good time.

To give myself time to think I took a sip of wine, the distinctive light floral-fruity bouquet overlaid with a hint of vanilla lingered on my tongue. "Do you come here often?" *Fool!* I cursed myself for using the age-old chat up line but this might be my only chance to discover all the personal details that were nagging away in the back of my mind.

Freya shook her head. "No, not often, I prefer to cook for myself. How about you?"

"Occasionally, most nights I make something simple at home, I don't go out very much these days."

I hadn't had a woman in my life for seven months. Not since Tricia, my lover of nine years walked off arm in arm with a butch firefighter she met on the internet. I'd spent the intervening time alone, licking my wounds, preferring my solitary lifestyle over having to break in somebody new. Until tonight, and Freya's advent, I hadn't actively considered changing my loveless state.

"Nor me." Freya sighed. "I'm still paying off my student loans, I can't afford to spend money on too many nights out until I've cleared some of the debt. But enough about me." She nailed me with a bewitching gaze that fired arrows of need straight into my core. "Tell me what you do."

"I'm a self-employed–"

Dino's arrival with our food silenced me. As was his custom he spent several minutes fussing over us, arranging the dishes to his satisfaction, talking all the while in his voluble mix of English heavily overlaid with his native Italian. Then he offered freshly shaved parmesan and pepper and wished us *"buon appetito"* before he scurried back to preside over his open plan kitchen.

The savory aroma teased my stomach into growling awareness, I dug into the fragrant pasta with my fork and Freya did likewise.

We said nothing more until we pushed our empty plates away, Freya a few seconds after me. "Mmmm, that was so good." She wiped her mouth with the napkin then leant back and her hand dropped down to rest lightly on my thigh. "You didn't finish telling me what you do."

Jeez! I could hardly think straight with her hand burning into my thigh like a branding iron. I sucked in a deep calming breath and forced the words out in a rush. "I...I'm a graphic designer."

"What do you design? Who are your clients? How−" She stopped abruptly and gave a soft laugh. "Sorry to be so inquisitive but it always bothers me seeing you all on your own in that big empty office with nobody to talk to."

"Mainly logos and promotional material for small businesses. I use the computer to work on the designs so there isn't anything obvious to show what I do."

Freya cocked her head and smiled. "I must come across tomorrow and you can demonstrate your skills." Her hand moved on my thigh giving me the distinct impression that her words held a double meaning.

A tangle of confused emotions crashed through my mind and evaporated like bubbles before I could capture them. "Yes, I'd like that." I had this sudden vision of me pulling down the blinds before pinning her naked body across the big desk that I never used, and then...

What was I thinking?

The unexpected nature of our meeting and our reaction to each other was amazing. Since Tricia's departure I'd sworn off all relationships even casual sex. I'd never been fond of one-nighters anyway, so the strength of my attraction to this woman confused me beyond reason. Granted we hadn't done anything, yet... but I'd been mooning over Freya for two months and now I'd learnt it was a case of mutual attraction I longed to dive in and take her. The voice of reason, however, bellowed at me to stop this now. I wasn't the right woman for her. All I could offer was a brief affair, a glorious one or maybe two night stand. She deserved better than that. A beauty like Freya needed emotional commitment, love and devotion something I was no longer able to provide. I silently cursed Tricia for her betrayal and the legacy she'd left in her wake.

I turned towards my companion, intending to put an end to this madness before it got out of hand. "Freya..."

Her lips parted on a sigh. "Yes?" The intensity with which she met my gaze sent a chain reaction of sensations through my body and drove all the breath from my lungs.

"We need to..." I stopped. I couldn't bring myself to say the words, to halt this emotional juggernaut that had seized control of my life.

"I know." Freya leant closer and whispered in my ear. "Let's get out of here before we cause a public outrage. We could go to my place, it's just across the square."

Tempting though her suggestion was, I still hesitated. My heart and body urged me to move, to go with her, to explore the possibilities and see where it led us, while my head voiced words of caution. This was all happening way too fast. Although I'd watched her from afar, it had never occurred to me that we'd actually get it on together.

Freya made the decision for me. She opened her purse and tossed a handful of bills on the table then pushed me along the seat until I had no choice but to stand or fall off the end.

I stood.

When Freya joined me, her gaze sought mine, imploring. I couldn't move or breathe for the emotion choking me. Then she took my hand. "Come." She urged me to move, dragging me through the crowded restaurant and out into the night. The storm had passed, leaving the warm night air filled with a soft perfume of flowers and trees. The gentle splash of the fountain, a defining feature of this small town, played softly in the background.

We got half way across the deserted square before Freya halted abruptly and pulled me into the shadow of a large statue. "Oh, Laura. I can't wait another second." She flung her arms around my neck and sealed her lips to mine. I surrendered to the incredible moment our tongues met. Freya tasted divine, a combination wine and the sweet vanilla gelato we'd shared for desert, but I wanted more than this drugging kiss. I wanted all of her at my mercy, our naked bodies melded together, to hear her screaming my name and begging me to fuck her and make her come.

Impatient to get the party started I spun her around and pushed her back against the marble plinth. My hands slid down to cup her ass and press her closer to me, if that were possible. Freya responded with a soft moan into my mouth and ground her pelvis hard against mine. I lifted her up until she got the message and wrapped her legs around me. Her short skirt crumpled easily around her hips, I slid one hand down between her thighs and probed the damp fabric of her panties. A tremor rippled through her body or was it mine? I couldn't tell I was too far gone. I pushed the flimsy barrier aside, her juices guiding my path to her slit. She immediately spasmed around my fingers drawing them deep into her silken depths. My head swam and my body ached with desire. I pumped her hard, wanting, needing to exert my butch authority by making her come for me, right here, right now.

Freya responded to my movements, working her slick pussy on my fingers. "Ahhh," she moaned softly. Seizing the initiative away from me she moved faster and harder, her breathing ragged. I felt her orgasm building.

The slam of car doors followed by laughter and approaching footsteps brought me to my senses. I snatched my fingers from her pussy and smothered her gasp of protest with my lips. "Shush," I murmured against her mouth. Then quickly lowered Freya to her feet and eased her skirt down her thighs seconds before two young couples walked past us.

My blood ran cold. Where was my sense? We'd almost got caught having sex in a public place. This small, narrow-minded, Southern town certainly wasn't ready for such an outrage.

"Oh my." Freya giggled, clearly enjoying the situation far more than me. "That was a close call."

A brief blast of live music shattered the silence as the group entered Donohue's Irish pub on the far side of the square.

I pulled away from her and shook my head. "Too close for comfort."

"Come on, Laura." Freya's eyes sparkled like diamonds against a night sky, reflecting the lights illuminating the fountain. "Where's your sense of adventure? Half the fun of fucking in a public place is taking a risk, and knowing you might get caught. It heightens the sexual excitement."

I avoided her as she made a grab for me. "Not for me, I prefer more certainty and an element of privacy. How close is your place?" My sexual drive didn't need any help from risk taking or danger.

"Spoilsport." Freya grinned and waved vaguely across the square toward the block that included Donohue's. "We're almost there." She dropped a light kiss on my lips then took my hand. I didn't need any further encouragement, I couldn't wait to get her naked and explore every last inch of her body. We sprinted the final hundred yards and I got a terrific view of her neat little ass as she ran ahead of me up the narrow staircase to her front door.

Her apartment, situated above a florists shop a few doors away from the noisy pub, was surprisingly quiet. Once inside she kicked the door shut with her heel then moved right into my arms. A storm of unbearable tension gripped my body. I spun her around, pinned her up against the wood and rained kisses down her throat.

She moaned as my lips reached the soft swell of her breast and my tongue dipped into her cleavage. I took that as a sign of encouragement and slid my hand inside her bra to lift one breast to my lips. My teeth grazed her rock-hard nipple and I felt the shockwave spread through her body like a series of minor earthquakes. She was so damned kissable in every area, I needed to get her naked, fast, so I could feast on the rest of her body. I reached around, to unclip her bra then whipped it and her tunic off in one movement. Next I unzipped her skirt. Then slid my hands down her thighs along with her skirt and thong. Freya stepped out of both on my direction then I sat back on my heels and surveyed my naked prize.

Freya stood before me, feet slightly apart, wearing nothing but a pair of sexy high heels. She met my gaze, her eyes luminous and her pupils dilated. Then she circled her lips with the tip of her tongue. The provocative action set my blood pressure soaring. My gaze swept down to her breasts, nipples standing proud from dark aureoles, over her flat stomach adorned with a jeweled butterfly navel ring and matching tattoo to her shaven mound. Pink and plump, and so damned sexy, like a ripe velvety peach just waiting to be plucked.

I licked my lips and reached up to sweep my tongue over her breasts lingering a while to circle and tease each nipple. Then I worked my way very slowly downward. Freya's body came alive in response as my lips and hands caressed her silken skin. I carefully avoided the one place I longed to taste, wanting to make this last. To imprint every inch of her into my memory for ever.

My lips traveled all the way back up her body.

"Please God!" I trapped her whimper with a kiss, my tongue delving deep into her sweet mouth, while my hands moved to cup her gorgeous breasts.

Not be outdone Freya tore at my shirt. A rat-tat-tat sound, like rapid rifle fire, filled the air as buttons flew in all directions ricocheting off the walls and floor. I didn't care that in her haste she ripped the buttons off rather than undo them then her fingers found the fastening on my sports bra and it went the same way.

I relinquished her breasts just long enough for her to drag the shirt down off my arms then my thumbs returned to the enjoyable task of caressing her nipples. The knowledge that my touch had produced these hard, eager buds did incredible things to my body and my ego.

Freya moaned softly and turned her attention to my jeans. She popped the button and dealt quickly with the zipper before pushing them and my boxers down until they fell around my ankles. I kicked my boots off and stepped out of the confining clothes then pushed them aside.

Naked, breathless, and beyond the point of control. Each sweep of my fingers over her silky skin wafted a warm floral perfume into the mix of our musky sexual need and increased my desire to press forward. I needed above all to touch her, to caress her skin with my lips, and to find a way to ease the excruciating pain of waiting to discover how sweet she tasted and how many beautiful sounds I could draw from her lips when she came for me.

Freya squirmed against me signaling her raging desire. "Please God, Laura, I need to come..." She reached for my hand, dragged it down and pressed it hard against her sweet mound. "I need you to fuck me, now."

I abandoned her mouth and trailed feverish kisses down her throat, skimmed along her collarbone, and then traveled lower until I reached her breasts. My lips sought her nipple and I felt a shudder tumble through her body as she thrust forward to greet my mouth.

My fingers eased between her thighs and found her slit. So hot, so wet, so sexy. I wanted to fuck her longer, harder, faster, than I'd ever wanted to fuck anybody before. She sunk her teeth into my neck. I almost climaxed. My thighs were slick with the hot juices flooding my pussy but I managed to control myself and hold back the tide.

I grazed her nipple with my teeth and her internal muscles contracted tightly around my digits drawing them deeper. Freya's wild gyrations proved too much, our balance gave out and we ended up on the floor, in a wild tangle of arms and legs, with my fingers buried deep inside her pussy. I fucked her slowly, forcing myself to take my time, to make the moment count. My fingers moved relentlessly in and out, almost withdrawing then plunging deep and hard, while I kissed and nibbled my way down her body, trying to memorize every single nuance to my progress.

Drawn by her heat and musky aroma I finally arrived at my destination. Her clit glistened like a precious jewel. I parted her lips and teased it with the very tip of my tongue then drew it deep into my mouth.

"Oh!" Freya's hips lifted off the floor. "Yes!"

Yes, indeed! My own pussy throbbed with every buck of Freya's slender hips. I knew exactly how she felt. For months I'd dreamed of this moment, of finding a way to cleanse all the hurt from my system, of gaining relief in a quick, powerful and explosive fuck. However, now the moment was here, I just wanted to drag out the conclusion and make it last forever.

Freya moaned in protest when my fingers slid from her pussy then sighed contentedly as my tongue took over the task of fucking her and my slick fingers found her clit.

She tasted divine, like I knew she would. Sweet as honey. Unwilling to delay any longer, I pushed her thighs up and apart, opening her fully, sinking my tongue deeper into her slit while massaging her clit.

All too quickly a scream tore from Freya's lips. Her body pulsed with the force of her orgasm. Hot, sweet, cream flooded like nectar onto my tongue as I drove her to the precipice then over the edge, draining her completely.

"Oh…" Freya sighed contentedly, her body relaxed, her labored breathing returning to normal. I kissed my way back up her body until I could cover her lips with mine. She opened her mouth, inviting me inside and our tongues intertwined in an intimate kiss.

We lay in contented silence for several minutes then Freya suddenly came alive. She pushed me over onto my back, straddled my hips and then sat back on her heels. "My turn." She grinned mischievously, before she leant forward to kiss my throat, her breath hot on my sensitive skin, she sucked and nibbled at the soft flesh below my ear.

Then she moved lower to close her lips over one nipple and almost catapulted me into orbit. Her soft hair teased my tits and sent erotic tingles fizzing through my body. I threaded my fingers into her hair pulling her tight and surrendered to the roller coaster ride of sensation.

I struggled to keep my sanity when her fingers eased between my thighs and dipped into my wetness. She plunged two fingers deep into my aching slit then, after a few moments, added a third, and then a fourth. The tips of her fingers grazed my g-spot each time she withdrew and her thumb caught my clit with each return thrust.

My orgasm built as she pushed deeper and harder. Her fingers felt so good, so right, filling me to perfection. Freya seemed to know instinctively what I wanted and what turned me on. My muscles contracted, eagerly anticipating the wonderful sensations to come. Then she came to a full stop.

"Please..." I begged her, straining for that extra movement that would grant me the relief my body craved.

She kept me waiting. Taking time to savor my tits with her lips and teeth. Then she began to move again, driving hard and fast then slow, varying her thrusts, until she plucked an orgasm from my tense body. Hot steel fingers of exquisite pain clawed at my insides, cramping them into a tight knot, before I shattered, screaming my relief as the world dissolved into an unimaginable kaleidoscope of rainbow lights against my closed eyelids.

She continued her thrusts long after I stopped pumping around her hand, drawing out every last quiver, until my body stilled completely.

Suddenly tears filled my eyes.

Why?

I never cried, it wasn't a very butch thing to do.

Had Freya somehow found my Achilles heel?

Keeping my face averted so she wouldn't witness

my moment of weakness I blinked hard until the flow of scalding liquid clouding my vision eased and I regained some measure of composure.

"Mmmm!" I rolled her over onto her side and kissed her lips, her throat, her breasts and then back up to her lips. "That was absolutely sensational. I haven't…it's been a long time…"

"Shush." Freya chuckled softly against my lips. "It's not over yet." She got up and pulled me to my feet. "Now I've caught you I don't plan on letting you escape any time soon. Let's go to bed, right now I desperately need you to fuck me again, we can talk all you want tomorrow or the next day."

I let her lead me by the hand hardly daring to believe that Freya's words offered the promise of a future beyond this one night of passion.

Lydian Press

About the Author

Dalia Craig loves to both read and write a variety of contemporary fiction. While her particular leaning is toward lesbian romance, her writing encompasses all heat levels and diverse genre. She has a number of eBooks to her credit and is also a contributor to several print anthologies including: Where the Girls Are: Urban Lesbian Erotica, Best Lesbian Romance 2010 both from Cleis Press. Plus the Goldie 2013 nominated anthology, Sapphic Planet, edited by Beth Wylde & Kissa Starling.

She published many short stories in eBook format with loveyoudivine Alterotica, where she was also managing editor for the FemErotica line until loveyoudivine closed in June 2013.

Dalia has wide and varied interests but mainly she loves to write. She is quoted as saying, "Writing is my life. It is what fulfils me as a person."

Aside from writing, Dalia loves to travel, fiddle with computers, listen to classical music, cook, grow her own fruit and vegetables, and befriend the wildlife that visits her garden.

You can connect with her online at: daliacraig.com

Lydian Press is dedicated to bringing you the finest GLBTQ erotic literature on the web.

Visit us on the web at:

http://lydianpress.com